Homecoming
Hometown Hearts
Holly Jacobs

Reviews:

Four Star Review: *"This is a heartwarming story about the power of second chances."*
—RTBookreviews

"...Jacobs is my favorite romance writer. Her characters lead ordinary lives...as people with problems, yearning for love."
—Lesa's Book Critiques

Homecoming... *"is going straight to my keeper shelf. I think it's the best writing she's ever done."* —The Romance Dish

Homecoming *"...is another wonderful family love story that reminds me once again, families can be anything we want them to be."*
—Kwips And Kritiques

Homecoming

Ilex Books
ISBN: 978-1-948311-06-9
Copyright © 2020 by Holly Fuhrmann

Previously Published as:
HOMECOMING DAY
ISBN: 978-1-4268-7646-2
Copyright © 2010 by Holly Fuhrmann

Dear Reader,

I have always been a reader. I tell people that I was raised by Tolkien, Lewis and Heinlein, and I'm only half kidding. Their stories—along with so many others—have taught me so much about acceptance and faith. And about love. Living my life without reading? I'd miss so much.

That's why my character JT's functional illiteracy was so compelling to me. According to the National Right to Read Foundation, "42 million American adults can't read at all and 20 percent of high school seniors can be classified as being functionally illiterate at the time they graduate." As a writer, I find these figures tragic; as a lifelong reader, I think they are a crime.

Despite that heavy subject, the real theme of the story is that life gives second chances...and sometimes so does love.

The last thing Laura Watson is looking for is love. She's lost her fiancé, had his baby...she just wants peace. But when Seth Keller comes into her life, she finds love. So does he, and he's not looking for it either. But finding love and embracing it are two different things. It takes a certain strength. And that's the question for both

Laura and Seth. Are they strong enough to take a chance on love again?

I hope you enjoy their journey and the rest of my *Hometown Hearts* series.

Holly Jacobs

Hometown Hearts
1. Crib Notes
2. A Special Kind of Different
3. Homecoming
4. Suddenly a Father
A Hometown Hearts Wedding
5. Something Borrowed
6. Something Blue
7. Something Perfect

Homecoming
Hometown Hearts

Holly Jacobs

To all my social media friends...
you all give me glee!

PROLOGUE

LAURA WATSON WATCHED the monitor.

The staff had long since turned down the volume, but she could still see the numbers rise and fall on the screen over Jay's head. Blood pressure. Heart rate. Those numbers should have been comforting. They meant Jay was still here with her.

But she knew those numbers were a lie. Despite the fact that Jay's heart was beating, he was gone.

His mother and father stood on the other side of the bed, their faces as ashen as Laura suspected her own was. His mother clutched his unmoving hand.

"We need to honor..." Laura's voice broke. She took a moment and tried again. "We need to honor Jay's wishes."

They were the hardest words that Laura had ever said. But she knew it was the right thing to do. It was what Jay would have wanted. It was what he made her promise.

Not that he'd planned this.

Jay was a cop and even in a small city like Erie, Pennsylvania, there was always a chance that he'd end up here in a hospital and this decision would be on her shoulders.

As they'd planned their future, planned their wedding, they'd discussed everything, including this possibility. Jay didn't want to linger, held to this life by machines.

But, despite all their conversations about the future, they hadn't envisioned this, because it wasn't a bullet that put Jay here. It was bacterial meningitis. Jay wasn't laid low in the line of duty, but by a tiny bacterium.

"He's not coming back," Laura said. "The doctors were clear."

Even if his body could survive this illness, his mind was gone and he'd never be Jay again.

They'd never be married. Their June wedding, only two weeks away, would never happen. No minister would ever pronounce them husband and wife. Jay would never know this child.

Laura's hands rested on her still-flat stomach. And this baby would never know its father.

The thought was a physical pain that tore at her.

She remembered the night she told him about her suspicions. They were engaged and already planning a fall wedding, but she'd still felt nervous, afraid that he'd be unhappy about a baby coming so soon.

She remembered his whoop of joy as he'd hurried across the room, scooped her up and swung her around in his excitement.

She remembered his moment of concern as he realized he was swinging around a pregnant woman.

She remembered his tender kiss and his assurances that this baby was welcome, wanted and was already loved. He'd been the one who'd urged her to push the wedding forward. He'd held her and whispered that he loved her and their child so much, he couldn't wait until fall.

The memory burned brightly. Tears streamed down her face. She'd fallen in love with Jay all over again. That's how it was with Jay. Every time she thought she loved him as much as humanly possible, he'd do something that would make that love grow exponentially.

"I hope she's beautiful like her mom, both inside and out. Blond hair and blue eyes," he'd whispered. "Smart, creative, sweet..." He'd kissed her cheek after each descriptive word, as if punctuating it.

She touched her cheek, willing herself to feel the imprint of his lips there, but it had long since gone cold.

Now, weeks later, she looked at Jay's parents, her unborn baby's only grandparents. Since she and Jay weren't married yet, his parents were the ones who would have to sign the papers that would allow the staff to remove the life support.

"He made it clear that it's what he wanted," she told them gently.

Jay's mother's face was suddenly animated with anger. "We won't pull the plug, Laura. You can't ask it of us."

"Mrs. Martin, the doctors said he's not going to recover, knowing what his job might entail, Jay was clear—"

Adele Martin was a tiny, elfin-looking woman who'd been so much more than her fiancé's mother or Laura's future mother-in-law. Laura loved her. But looking at her now, so upset, Laura admitted she didn't really know her at all. Laura was taken aback by Mrs. Martin's rage.

"You have no idea how hard a parent will fight for a child, for a miracle," Jay's mother said. "I'm not giving up on my son just because you have."

"Mrs. Martin, I haven't given up on anything." Nothing except her heart and her dreams. "I—"

"Get out, Laura. Go. My husband and I will look after Jay. We don't need you here."

Laura stared at the woman—the woman who'd asked her to call her Mom. Laura recalled laughing and telling Adele, *After the wedding, when it's official.* When she'd said those words, she'd planned on a life with Jay, and his parents becoming her parents. Finally, after years of being on her own, she'd belong to someone—to a family. She could still see the fragments of that imagined future. And the knowledge that it would never happen was crushing.

Her heart broke as she pushed back the chair and stood, facing the Martins. She knew there wasn't anything left she could do for Jay except honor this one last request and she didn't have the power to do it. "He didn't want this."

She leaned down and kissed his still-warm cheek. It would be so easy to deceive herself. To watch the machine and believe its lie—believe that Jay was there and that somehow they'd still have a life together.

Filled with sorrow, she said goodbye to the family she'd hoped to belong to, then turned and walked from the room.

Laura realized that the idea of the family she'd wanted was an illusion.

But this baby growing inside her—her child and Jay's—was the reality. And the family she'd build with the baby would be real, too.

CHAPTER ONE

LAURA WATSON COULDN'T SAY being in Erie City Hall was the last place on earth she wanted to go, but it was close. Actually, the last place was the warren of offices nestled in the back of the building.

Her long brown coat fluttered against her pants as she strode down the hall, thankful at least to be out of the November cold. Erie, Pennsylvania, was set on the edge of the Great Lake that shared its name. Winter hit early and hard as the cold Canadian air blew across the lake's open water. She reached the police department's door and gripped the handle a little too tightly, a little too long, before pulling the heavy door open.

She could do this.

The baby in her stomach kicked, as if in agreement, affirming that she could. Reminding her that she wasn't alone.

Laura rested her hand on the top of her huge stomach. It now stretched her coat to its capacity. She only had four or five weeks left of her pregnancy, but already she was missing knowing that her baby would be with her always, and always safe.

She knew that life was uncertain. Once her baby was born, there were so many things that could go wrong, both physically and emotionally. She could do everything in her power to protect him or her, but in the end, her best might not be good enough.

The image of Jay in that hospital bed flashed through her mind as it had daily these last six months.

She pushed the image aside. Right now she had to focus on other things.

Laura made her way into the small anteroom. There was a counter with a glass barrier separating her from those on duty.

"Can I help you?" The woman at the desk closest to the counter got up and moved toward her.

Laura felt a wave of gratitude that she didn't know the clerk. Maybe her luck would hold out and she wouldn't see anyone she knew. Most of patrol would be out on the street, and she didn't know many of the support staff. "I'm here about Jillian Thomas."

The woman consulted a file in front of her, and then looked up at Laura. "Are you her mother?"

Laura shook her head. "No, I'm her teacher. Her mom's on her way, but JT—Jillian—asked me to come down and wait with her. I suspect she's afraid."

The clerk nodded and smiled sympathetically. "I suspect that you're right. Let me get someone to show you where she is."

Laura noticed the wall of pictures. Fallen officers. Her stomach twisted in knots for the families they'd left behind. Jay might not have died in the line of duty, but she knew the pain of losing someone. She wouldn't wish that on anyone.

She'd spent hours trying to remember every detail of their last night together. Jay had been on third shift, which meant he didn't have to be into work until ten at night. They'd had dinner together. Spaghetti. She'd pulled out her wedding file and showed him her seating chart and they'd talked about the ceremony they'd advanced because of the baby. They were to be married in two weeks.

She'd told him about the doctor's appointment that day, and they talked about going out with friends. They'd talked about childbirth and parenting classes.

A little before ten, he'd kissed her goodbye. She'd tried to remember exactly what time, but couldn't. And the fact that she couldn't bothered her. She knew it was probably about nine-thirty. That's the time he generally left. But was it nine twenty-nine or nine thirty-one? She should know. She should be able to remember.

Jay had kissed her, but he'd never mentioned a headache, or not feeling well. That was the next morning when he'd come home.

That last night had been normal. A prelude of all the nights they anticipated having together.

Years. Decades worth of nights like that. Of dinners and conversations about little bits of nothing. A chance to reconnect and share their lives—even the most trivial parts—at the end of the day.

Fate had stolen her lifetime of moments with Jay.

"Miss?" A male officer with very short light brown hair and a nice smile opened the door to the right of the reception desk.

Laura felt an immediate wave of relief. She didn't know this officer, either. He looked familiar in a vague sort of way. Maybe she'd seen him at the police picnic, or maybe she'd spotted him last April when Jay's car had been in the shop and she'd driven him to work for a week. Or maybe she recognized him from the long line of officers who had filed into the funeral home to pay their last respects to Jay and his family. But whoever he was, he wasn't anyone she knew. He wasn't one of Jay's good friends.

"Hi—" she glanced at the bars on his uniform "—Lieutenant. I'm here about Jillian Thomas."

The officer was maybe three or four inches taller than her and the military cut of his hair might have made him look severe if it wasn't for his eyes. They were a sort of golden-brown that softened the hard lines of his face. Right now, those eyes were staring at her, as if weighing her up, and Laura found herself wondering what he was thinking.

He didn't say, he simply finished his assessment, nodded and said, "Right. You're her teacher?"

"Yes. Her mom's coming, but JT asked me to be here and wait with her. I wasn't sure if you'd allow me to see her, or not, but I promised I'd come."

"We don't normally allow people to do so, other than the parents, but if you don't tell, I won't. This way." He smiled as he held a door for her. "I'm Seth. Lieutenant Seth Keller."

"Laura Watson," she replied. His name sounded familiar, but Laura still couldn't place it and for that, she was grateful.

"I'm the new liaison between the department and the school district," he said, answering her unasked question, as they walked down the hall.

Laura was too distracted to really register what he was saying. She felt exposed here. Any minute, from around any corner, someone Jay knew could appear. She didn't want to see any of his friends. Not that they weren't kind. They were. They were so kind and considerate that there were times Laura felt she'd suffocate from it all.

She'd tried to distance herself, but the men in Jay's group didn't take a hint.

She never knew what she'd find coming home from school. The lawn mowed, the leaves raked, the garbage cans carried to the curb.

She didn't even want to think about what it'd be like once the baby arrived. She'd done her best to dissuade their help, but Jay's friends kept on despite her protests.

Thankfully, the hallway was deserted. The lieutenant showed her into a small room with a long table and a few chairs. "I have her in here, waiting for her mom."

JT tossed the lieutenant a defiant look as they entered, then spotted Laura and surprise registered on her face. "You came?"

"Of course I did, JT."

"I wasn't sure you would, figured you'd track my mom down. The cops are having problems finding her. I don't think they're too bright," she added, with a mock whisper.

"Why don't I leave you two to talk," the lieutenant said, ignoring JT's comment.

Laura smiled at him. "Thanks."

"Sure." He nodded at her then shut the door behind him.

"It might be a while, Ms. Watson. Mom's got a new boyfriend, so she's busy."

JT's words might have sounded like a sneer to someone else, but Laura had been keeping an eye on the girl for weeks. There was something going on with her, and Laura wasn't sure what. JT was smart and talented. She excelled in

Laura's art classes, at least, she did when she bothered to show up.

"I'm sorry," Laura said. And she was. Sorry that JT was here. Sorry she was having problems. Sorry that she was obviously in pain and Laura didn't know how to help her.

Teens were supposed to feel angst. It seemed like a rite of passage. But whatever was happening with JT was more than normal teen moodiness, or even a kid adjusting to being in high school.

"Want to talk about it?" she asked, not for the first time. "This is more serious than skipping my class, or not turning in an assignment. And it looks like we have some time."

"I know. I know I was stupid to get in the car with Courtney. I wasn't drinking. You can ask that cop. They Breathalyzed me. No alcohol at all in my system. But I knew Courtney'd had a beer. I swear I didn't know she was drunk, if I did, I wouldn't have gotten into the car with her, but I'd've stopped her from driving, too. I could have taken her keys. I mean it, Ms. Watson. I never would have—"

"It's okay, JT. I believe you."

Her shoulders sagged, as if Laura's belief had eased something in her.

Laura studied the girl. JT was tiny. She didn't look as if she could be in high school, not even a freshman. She was maybe five feet tall. She'd shaved her auburn hair almost as short as the lieutenant's. She had a row of earring studs in each ear, one in the side of her nose, and a small hoop in her right eyebrow. And JT wore a lot of black. Today, she had on skintight black pants, a small T-shirt and black leather jacket.

"My mom's going to kill me," she said miserably.

"I'm sure she's going to punish you, but I doubt death will be involved."

JT's expression said she didn't believe a word Laura was saying. But she didn't say as much. Instead she asked, "So how are you feelin'? The kid's comin' soon, right?"

"I'm feeling fine, and the baby's fine, too. Thanks for asking."

"Did you get a room ready for it yet?"

"I'm working on it." The room was filled with boxes and bags. Laura had dutifully bought what the baby needed, but couldn't find the enthusiasm to assemble furniture, sort clothes or even decorate. Every time she thought about starting, she'd think of Jay, and how they'd planned on doing it together and she simply couldn't do it alone.

"It will get done in time," she said more for herself than to JT.

"I was thinking..." JT stood and pulled a sheet of paper out of her back pocket. "I mean, you do art, and I'm sure you've got the kid's room painted real cool, but if not, maybe you'd like something like this..." She shrugged, offered the paper to Laura, then turned away to stare at some indistinct point on the slate-gray wall.

Laura studied the well-worn piece of notebook paper. It looked as if JT had carried it around in her back pocket for a long time. The girl had sketched in a beautiful mural. There was a castle and, judging by their crowns, a princess and prince riding on horseback in a field that surrounded it.

"I figured if it was a girl, she should know right off that she can do anything a boy can do, and if it's a boy, he should learn that girls are just as good. Might save you some headaches later."

Laura chuckled as she continued looking at the sketch. There was a dragon setting a table for tea, and a tree that appeared to be growing... "Bubbles?" she asked, pointing.

JT nodded. "Yeah, anyone can paint an apple tree. But a bubble tree? Now that's something. I have this idea of iridescent paint and... Well, if you're interested."

"I'm more than interested, JT. I'm delighted. The baby would love it."

JT took the paper back, folded it along the creases and stuffed it in a pocket. "Well, maybe if I'm not grounded forever, I could do it for you as a baby gift."

"It would take a lot of time. And I know that you're behind in a few classes."

"I—"

Whatever JT was about to say was cut off by the woman who charged into the room. "JT, what the hell?"

"Mom, I wasn't drinking. You can ask him." She pointed at the lieutenant who was standing behind JT's mother in the doorway.

"The test said she wasn't, ma'am," he confirmed. "But she was in the car with a friend who had been drinking and was driving."

"You really work at making my life miserable, don't you? You're like your father. Two of a kind. Maybe it's his turn to take you." The woman paused, then said, "Oh, wait, he doesn't want you, either."

Laura was aghast that any mother would speak to her child like that. "Mrs. Thomas, I don't think that kind of talk is beneficial. Maybe—"

JT's mom ignored Laura and spoke over her, addressing the officer. "Can I take her now?"

The lieutenant nodded. "Yes, ma'am. You signed the papers, right?"

"Yeah, I signed your papers. Come on." JT's mother grabbed her arm and pulled her from the room. Laura picked up her purse and followed them down the hallway, not sure what else to do.

The lieutenant walked beside her, not saying anything.

They got outside and Laura saw Mrs. Thomas and JT climbing into their car. It was obvious they were fighting. But when Mrs. Thomas reached over and smacked JT, Laura's jaw dropped, as if she'd been the one who'd been slapped.

The lieutenant brushed by Laura and charged across the small parking lot. He knocked purposefully on the driver's side window. Laura couldn't hear what was said, but he leaned in and spoke earnestly to the woman for a minute, then stepped back as she pulled out of the parking space and drove onto the street.

A gust of cold wind blew by and he hurried toward the building.

"You let her go." Laura had wanted to chase after JT's mom as well, but given her size, walking was enough of a trial.

"There's nothing more I could do. It was only a slap, I'd be hard-pressed to make an abuse charge stick. The woman was disciplining her daughter." The lieutenant's words sounded calm, but there was a hint of something in his tone—something that said he was as upset at that slap as she was.

"I don't believe in hitting kids. Ever," he said. "But I don't write the laws. I simply enforce them. But I did tell her that I'd be checking in with JT next week at school. And you'll contact me if you see anything I can make stick." He reached into his shirt pocket and pulled out a business card. "Call me. Anytime."

"Thank you, Lieutenant."

Laura clutched the card as she started across the parking lot to her own car.

"Laura," came a voice that wasn't the lieutenant's. She recognized it and knew that her luck had run out. Every fiber of her being wanted to keep walking, but she didn't. She turned to face the man who reminded her of what Jay might have looked like if he'd lived to be his father's age.

"Sir."

Mr. Martin looked as if he'd aged a decade since Jay's funeral. She'd made it clear that she didn't want to see him or his wife, and they'd stayed away, though they called to ask about the baby's progress. The conversations were stilted and uncomfortable at best. But now, here he was and she'd been right, seeing him hurt.

"How are you?" he asked.

"The baby's fine," she answered, knowing that was his real question. Chief Martin wanted to know about his grandchild, not his son's almost-wife.

"We've missed you."

Laura looked at her watch. "I'm sorry. I have to go."

Knowing she was a coward, but not caring, she hurried to her car as quickly as she could given her ponderous size. And she purposefully didn't glance back at the man she'd once thought would be her father.

Her hand rested on her stomach. This baby was all the family she'd have.

And that was enough.

SETH WATCHED THE TALL BLONDE waddle to her car.

"Why was Laura here?" Chief Jameson Martin asked Seth.

The deputy chief's voice was choked with emotion, but Seth understood the unwritten code of manly conduct and ignored it. He simply answered his boss's question. "One of her students, Chief. Ms. Watson came to wait with her until the girl's mom picked her up."

"You gave her a card?"

Martin didn't miss a thing. "Yeah. She's worried about the girl. So am I. The mom smacked the kid, but I have no reason to suspect anything more than a parent at her wit's end. Still, I talked to the mom and I told Miss Watson to call me if she saw any evidence that there's more than an isolated slap going on." He paused and asked, "You know her?"

"She was Jay's fiancée."

Shit.

Seth knew Martin had lost his son last spring. He'd gone to Kloecker's Funeral Home, like the rest of the department. They'd all filed through, offering condolences, shaking hands, even hugging Mrs. Martin.

He remembered there was a fiancée, but he hadn't known until now that she was pregnant. And from her reaction, things were not very amicable between her and the chief. Seth wasn't sure what to say about it or what to do, so he stood and waited.

Martin finally spoke, breaking the silence. "She doesn't want anything to do with us. If we call, she's polite enough, but she's put a wall between us. It's killing my wife. That baby is our last connection to our son, but more than that, my wife loves Laura."

Seth was pretty sure it was killing Martin, too, but he didn't say it.

"I'm sorry." His mother once told him that there are some pains that are so great that those are the only words that can be offered. And yet, he wished he had something more to offer his chief. "Maybe she'll come around."

"I'd like to think she will, but..." Martin's voice cracked, and he was silent a moment. "You'll tell me if you see her again? If there's anything she needs, you'll let me know? A lot of guys from Jay's group have been taking care of some work around her house. Not that she asks. She keeps insisting she's fine. But how can she be?"

There were three patrol groups on the Erie Police Department. Martin's son, Jay, was assigned to a different group than Seth's. They'd known each other, but never worked together. Seth figured Jay's group would consider Laura Watson one of their own, as they should. Even if she insisted she didn't need their help, they'd help.

"Sure," he promised. "I've got to go into her school next week. Why don't I make it a point to check in with her about her student?"

"I'm not asking you to spy on her, or break any confidence," Martin assured him hastily. "It's that she's our only link left with Jay. Her and the baby. But it's more than that. We loved Laura as if she was our own. When we lost Jay, we lost her, too, and it hurt. We'd do anything for her, if she'd let us."

"Sure thing, Chief. I'll keep an eye on her."

He turned and walked back into the office, his mind on Laura Watson.

The very pregnant Laura Watson.

And that thought made him remember Allie. Not that he ever forgot her. She was there with him, every day. At first, Allie had been there every minute, a constant pain that ached with every breath he took. Now, that pain wasn't as fierce or frequent, but as it faded, he was left with this huge hole in his life. And he didn't know how to fill it.

He could understand Laura Watson's pain at losing her fiancé. Losing that one person you loved more than life itself—it was the kind of thing you never actually got over. You might learn to live, despite the loss. But you were never truthfully the same.

He shut off such thoughts. He was at work and couldn't afford the distraction. Later, tonight, he'd remember, and if he was lucky, he'd dream about Allie.

That's all he had left.

CHAPTER TWO

TUESDAY AFTERNOON, LAURA looked at the sullen girl wiping down the chalkboard. JT was not impressed that she was doing her detention with Laura instead of in the usual auditorium. While she was cooperating, she made her displeasure clear with every movement, every monosyllabic response.

Gone was the girl who'd called on her for help.

Laura ignored JT's mood. "When you're done with that, why don't you sit down and start your homework?"

"Yeah, whatever."

Laura had gone to the principal's office first thing Monday morning. She'd told him about the police station and had asked if JT could do her latest round of punishment with her rather than in the auditorium with the rest of the students. Mike Asti had readily agreed. "It doesn't seem like the normal route is working with JT. She's a C to D student with little academic motivation. And she's had daily detentions a lot this year. It's definitely not the most auspicious way to start a high school career. Maybe something a bit less traditional would help her," he said. "And let's face it, she's only a freshman, and so far every one of her teachers has complained about her, but you. Maybe she needs someone on her side."

Laura watched as JT stomped across the room, slumped into one of the desks and picked up a book. Their second day of detention wasn't going particularly well. Somehow, she intended to reach the girl.

Laura was mulling over what she should do about or say to JT, when someone knocked on the door.

JT jumped up as if she were going to see who it was.

"I've got it," Laura assured her. "You, homework."

JT slammed back into her seat with an audible thump.

Laura opened the door and found Lieutenant Keller standing in the hallway. His dark blue uniform was very starched and perfectly pressed. She'd noticed his eyes at the police station the other night, and was drawn to them again this afternoon. But this time it wasn't their golden-brown color that softened his whole look, it was his expression—a sort of look that said, *you can trust me.*

She'd hazard a guess that small children gravitated to him. She could imagine them spilling their secrets and showing him their treasures, and he'd take it all in with a sincere interest.

She realized she'd been silently studying him longer than was polite. "Lieutenant, what can I do for you?"

"I'm looking for JT. I said I'd stop in and check on her."

Laura nodded her head toward the student who was hiding behind a book.

Seth raised his eyebrows questioningly toward the girl. Laura realized he was asking if she minded if he talked to her. She smiled, silently giving him her permission.

Seth entered the classroom and folded himself gingerly into the desk next to JT's. "Hi, JT. I'm Lieutenant Keller from the other night."

"Yeah, I remember. Once a guy locks you up, he sort of becomes memorable. I went home and pulled out my very pink diary and wrote, *Dear Diary, guess who I met tonight?*"

"*You know, you can lie to other people, but you should never lie to yourself or your diary. What you should have written was, Dear Diary, This very nice, understanding and probably very intelligent cop put me in a waiting room after I made a boneheaded decision.*"

Laura thought she saw a ghost of a smile flit across JT's face, but it was so fast she couldn't be sure.

The girl simply scowled at the police officer and shrugged. "Yeah, whatever."

Seth didn't appear phased by her sullenness, but forged ahead. "I was worried about you and wanted to be sure everything's okay at home."

"What you're asking is if my mom beats me? I mean, you saw the slap in the car and you're worried that I'm abused. But no, she doesn't beat me or abuse me in any way. Ms. Watson asked, too. I'll tell you what I told her, my mom's not interested enough to beat me. She was annoyed that I'd ruined her date, that's all."

"I'm sure—"

JT cut him off. "So am I. I am utterly positive that my mother doesn't beat me. I'm not abused. Ignored, maybe, but I don't think that's a crime. Listen, Officer, I'm fine. Mom slapped me 'cause she was pissed. She went back to her date and forgot all about it. She even forgot to ground me. So, don't worry. You've done your duty." She glanced at the clock. "And so have I. Detention's over, so I'm gonna go. Okay, Ms. Watson?"

Laura glanced at the clock and nodded. "Yes. I'll see you here after school tomorrow."

"Yeah, whatever." JT gathered up her books, stuffed them in her backpack and rushed out of the room.

Laura waited for the door to slam before she apologized to the officer. "Sorry she was rude, Lieutenant—"

He unfolded himself from the desk and corrected her. "Seth."

"Seth," Laura agreed. "It was nice of you to check on her."

"Listen, I know it's a bit early, but I want to grab something to eat before I head for the station. Want to get a slice of pizza at Porky's and we can talk about JT?"

Laura wasn't sure she wanted to at all. As a matter of fact, she was pretty positive she didn't. Porky's was close to City Hall and frequented by the entire police department. She didn't want to run into any of Jay's friends, but she did want the lieu—Seth, she corrected herself. She felt something ease in her as she altered his name in her head. It was easier to think of him as Seth than as a lieutenant.

And Porky's or not, she did want his advice on JT.

She missed having Jay to bounce things off of. Problems with students. The small triumphs. None of the other teachers had been overly interested in JT. Most had decided she was a problem student, and a few had totally written her off. Seth seemed genuinely concerned, so maybe he'd have an idea. "Sure. I'll follow you there."

SETH WASN'T SURE WHAT possessed him to invite Laura to join him for dinner, but he was glad she'd accepted the offer. He was also glad to see her in an all-wheel drive vehicle, which he'd noted on their way to Eighth and Myrtle. It might be only early November, but that wasn't too soon to think about winter. And the winters in Erie could be brutal. Some people in town drove cars that simply weren't suited to the climate. But not only was the all-wheel drive suitable, the cherry-red color suited her somehow, too.

He kept glancing in his rearview mirror. Stopped at a red light, he blatantly stared at her. It appeared that Laura was a singer, and whatever song was playing must be a favorite because she wasn't merely singing, but doing a little head-bop, as well.

He couldn't help smiling as she parked behind him at a meter. He waited and walked across the street with her.

"What are you grinning at?" she asked.

"So, what song was playing?"

"Huh?"

"Something you like was on the radio as we drove here."

She laughed. "Ha! Jay used to tease me about my car-singing habits. And rumor has it I'm just as bad in the shower."

She froze as she said the word shower, as if she'd shared something too personal.

"So, what song?"

"Lady Antebellum's 'Looking for a Good Time.'"

"A country fan," he commented, as they entered the small pizza joint.

"Do you mind if we sit in the corner?" she asked.

"Sure." He led her to one of the vacant tables. "I'll go place our order. Anything in particular?"

"I'm not picky."

Normally, Seth would choose a traditional pepperoni pizza, but given Laura's condition, he asked for a vegetable pizza instead and brought them both bottles of water.

"So, tell me more about JT," he said.

"I teach art. I'm sure you guessed that when you walked into my classroom. Anyway, JT's a freshman and she's got talent. A lot of talent. I've so enjoyed having her in my class, but the other teachers..."

"Not so much?" he supplied.

"Not so much," she agreed. She took off her coat and rested her arms on top of her huge stomach. "She rarely turns in homework and her classroom behavior isn't much better. She's passing, but only just."

Seth forced his gaze upwards and concentrated on Laura's face. It had been easy to forget about her pregnancy when she was bundled up. "So she's doing detention with you?"

"I went to the principal Monday morning and requested it." She continued recounting her conversation and concluded with, "We hope maybe a stint with me might give me the opportunity to find out what's really going on with her. Possibly give her a chance to open up to someone."

"You must be reaching her on some level. After all, she did call you when she was waiting for her mom."

Laura nodded. "Yes, there's that. Although, it's not like she's said a lot that night or this week."

"So the strategy is to wait it out and try to get her to talk." It was a statement, not a question. Seth hardly knew Laura, but he knew this much about her.

"Yes."

"Is there something I can do?"

"I'd take any advice you have. I'm at my wit's end."

"Just keep caring about her. Sometimes it simply takes one person caring to help a kid turn a corner."

"Two," she said.

"Two?"

"You care, too. You stopped by today to check on her because you care, so she's got two of us in her corner."

"It's my job."

She shook her head, looking as if she didn't believe him.

"It is," he protested. "A good cop's goal isn't just to arrest someone, but to step in before they *have* to arrest someone."

She shook her head again. "It's more than your job, at least with JT. You see a lot of troubled kids. You stopped by today because she's more than a job for you."

"I could say the same thing about you," he pointed out. "I'll be the first to admit, we can't save everyone, but we can save some. I have a sister, Cessy, who's only a few years older than JT. I would hope that if she had problems, someone would step in and help her if I couldn't be there for her."

The pizza came and they each chose a slice.

After a couple bites, Laura asked, "Is your family here in Erie?"

Not a topic he wanted to discuss, but he answered, "No, not Erie proper. They're in Whedon."

Seth had grown up in Whedon, a small town just outside of Erie. But he'd joined the Erie police force because it was bigger and offered a lot more opportunities to advance.

"That's nice that your family's so close," Laura said.

It didn't seem as if they were close at all. The mere fifteen minutes distance might as well have been hours or days. Seth hadn't felt connected to his family in years.

No, that wasn't right. He still felt connected to his siblings. It was his parents he was no longer close to. And the irony was, he loved them. But their estrangement had gone on for so long he didn't know how to fix it.

"How many siblings?" Laura asked.

He smiled when he thought of his eclectic family. "There are six of us. My parents adopted us—" He stopped, unsure why he'd felt the need to share that. "You?"

"Just me. An only child of two only children."

Seth couldn't imagine what that was like. He had friends who came from big families, and most of them said they dreamed of being an only child. Not Seth. His family, the way it was, had been his dream. It was a dream that he sometimes thought he'd lost, and that hurt. Worse, he was unsure what he could do to get it back.

Truthfully, he didn't want to think about his family or his past. He'd spent the last few years perfecting each as an art form. Concentrating on Laura was easier. Not that he was spying on her for the chief. But if he could put his commander at ease, without betraying Laura's confidence in him, he would.

"Do your parents live in town?" he asked conversationally.

"My mom died when I was in fourth grade. After that it was me and Dad. He passed away right after I started college. Sometimes I think he held out long enough to be sure I could take care of myself before he felt he could join her."

"I'm sorry."

"Me, too," Laura admitted. "About JT, maybe between the two of us we can get her to open up."

They chatted about Laura's classes and he described his new job as liaison to the school district. She listened to him talk about his hopes for the position as they ate their pizza. Stunned that they'd been talking for more than forty-five minutes, he shoved his last bite of pizza into his mouth. "Laura, this has been great, but I've got to be at the station."

"Thanks for dinner, but more than that, thanks for caring, Lieutenant."

"I thought I was Seth now?" he reminded her.

"You are." Laura smiled as she repeated his name. "Seth. Thanks for following up with JT and for the pizza. Any night I don't have to cook is a bonus."

"I'll try to stop in and check on JT. Friday, if that works?"

"That would be nice."

"I'll see you then. Take the rest of the pizza home, would you? I hate to let it go to waste." He stood up.

Laura got up out of her chair. It was almost painful to watch her struggle onto her feet. "Sure. Feed the pregnant woman. That's what she needs."

He'd forgotten about her being pregnant and blanched at the reminder. "Friday. See you Friday." He bolted.

He knew that's what he'd done. It was cowardly. Still, seeing her reminded him of Allie. And even now, years later, it hurt.

And now he'd promised to visit Laura on Friday.

Way to go, Keller.

ON THURSDAY AT HER SECOND period freshman art class, Laura took attendance and discovered that JT wasn't there.

She toyed with Seth's card.

During her lunch break, she called the number and got his voice mail. "Hi, Seth. You said to let you know if I had any problems with JT. Well, she didn't come to school today. I'm going to head over to her house after school. I'll keep you posted." She was ready to hang up and then added, "Oh, I should have said, this is Laura."

She sighed. Of course he'd know it was her. Who else would have called about JT?

She tried the number listed on JT's contact form. No one answered.

By the time school ended, she gathered up her things and hurried out of the room. And ran right into Lieutenant Seth Keller's ample chest.

He jumped back as if he'd been burned, went beet-red and stammered, "Are you okay? The baby. I mean—"

"I'm fine. We're fine," she assured him.

"Where were you speeding to?" He pinned her with a look her father had often employed. One she suspected she'd need to learn as her baby grew up. The look said, *go ahead and answer, because I already know the answer, and I'm not pleased.*

The look had made her feel chagrined when her father had employed it, not so when Seth used it. "To JT's house, like I told you in that message. I'm worried that she didn't show up at school today."

"You were going by yourself?"

She nodded. Seth looked—well, he looked pissed. "Okay. Laura, I know I have no say in what you do, but—"

"You're right you have no say in anything I do."

She started walking down the hall and Seth dogged her heels, which she expected wasn't all that hard considering her girth. She already felt winded, while he spoke in a nice, even measure. "Yeah, well, you're pregnant and arriving alone at the home of a student whose mother you know has a temper—does that seem wise?"

She stopped and hoped that he took the gesture as annoyance, not the fact she'd walked too fast and needed to catch her breath. To give herself a moment, she gave him a look she used on her students. It wasn't as intimidating as the paternal-look was, but it was the best in her arsenal. When she thought she could speak without huffing and puffing, she said, "Pardon me, Lieutenant, but when did you sign on as my keeper? I missed the paperwork on that."

"Obviously someone should watch out for you."

The words hit her and her annoyance evaporated, replaced by sadness. Seth was right. Someone should. Jay should be here, fussing over her, worrying about her worrying about JT. She missed him. Terribly. Sniffing, she surreptitiously swiped at her eyes.

"Are you crying?" Seth's voice rose in a rather uncoplike way.

She could distinctly hear the universal male horror at the thought of her tears. She lied when she said, "No," the catch in her voice giving herself away entirely.

"You are crying. I know you're crying. I've got three sisters, and I can tell crying when I hear crying."

The fact he'd witnessed his sisters' tears obviously hadn't hardened Seth to the sight.

She gave one more healthy sniff and blinked back the waterworks. "You've said the word *crying* more than any man—especially a cop—should. And you're wrong. I'm not crying. I have allergies. And I'm pretty sure the thing I'm most allergic to is you and your bossy ways."

"Right, allergies."

He was probably used to women hanging all over him and thought she was kidding. Well, she wasn't. She didn't need a keeper. "But let's be honest, I don't owe you any allergy explanations, and I certainly don't have to check in with you when I'm going about my business. So good afternoon, Lieutenant." She started down the hall.

Seth easily matched her pace.

"May I come, too?" he asked.

"Why?" she asked defensively. "To keep an eye on the pregnant woman who obviously doesn't have enough sense to take care of herself?"

"No, of course not. I want to come because I'm worried about JT, too."

She could have taken offense if he was trying to control or protect her, but she couldn't quite manage it if he was simply trying to help JT. She eyed him suspiciously. "Really?"

"Cops care, too." Then he smiled, held up a few fingers and said, "Policeman's honor."

She sighed. "Fine. I'll give you the address. You can meet me there." It wasn't the most gracious invitation, but she wasn't feeling overly gracious.

"Or."

"Or?" she repeated as she continued down the hall.

"Or, I could drive and bring you back afterward to pick up your car."

She wanted to say no. As a matter of fact, she wanted to say hell no. But instead, she found herself saying, "Fine." She was hopeless at directions. For her birthday last year, Jay had given her a GPS. She'd laughed, telling him she wasn't planning any out-of-town trips.

He'd responded he knew that. The GPS was for navigating around town.

And for the first time since he died, she remembered Jay and had an urge to laugh rather than cry.

She glanced at the quiet police officer next to her, and though he wore the same uniform, there weren't any other similarities to Jay.

Jay had worn his hair on the shaggy side of long, compared to Seth's military cut. And Jay had been quick to laugh. She hadn't seen any signs of quick laughter in Seth Keller. He'd smiled, but even then, the expression hadn't quite reached his eyes. He wasn't grim. He was more sad. She wondered what had happened to make him that way.

They walked in silence to the parking lot and he led her to a huge truck. It was blue and had one of the cabs that had a backseat with a second door. It also sat about a mile off the ground.

Somehow Laura needed to get her beached-whale self up and into it. She was pretty sure it was going to take a forklift. She was about to ask if maybe Seth would consider taking her car when he said, "Would you be offended if I offered you a hand?"

"I'm practical enough to admit I do need a hand."

He got her settled in the giant truck. She gave him JT's address and they drove in silence toward the nice section of town. Seth stopped in front of a neat, two-story brick house.

Laura slid out of the truck with more ease than she'd gotten in. She clutched the manila folder she'd put JT's homework sheets in, pulled her coat tight against her chest and waddled to the door with Seth at her side. He let her take the lead. She appreciated that.

She knocked and they waited. When no one answered, she rang the doorbell and called out, "JT, it's Ms. Watson, and I'm not going anywhere until you open the door. And it's very cold out here. I'm so huge that my coat doesn't want to button, so the baby bump sort of sticks out. I bet the baby's as cold as I am."

Yeah, using the baby was low, but if it got results, she wasn't above it.

Seconds later the door opened and JT stood there scrubbed bare of any makeup and wearing a pair of holey jeans and a pink, oversize sweatshirt that made her look so much younger than she did in school.

"Ms. Watson?"

Laura held out the envelope. "I brought your homework. Can we come in for a moment?"

JT jerked her finger in Seth's direction. "What's he doing here?"

"Lieutenant Keller stopped by and offered to bring me. He seems to think my absurd size makes it hard for me to reach the steering wheel and, therefore, I shouldn't drive any more than I have to."

"You are kinda big." JT's grin said she was teasing. "I mean, you're right, if you did up your coat, a button would probably pop off and become a lethal weapon."

Seth glommed on to JT's mood and said, "Now, when my sister-in-law Eli was pregnant, I thought she was big, but then I met Laura here. She gives the phrase big-as-a-house a whole new meaning."

"Hey, you two." Laura waved her hand and tried to look outraged. "I'm standing right here in my tight, unbuttoned coat."

JT grinned. "Yeah, big as a McMansion for sure."

Seth laughed. "I was thinking castle, but your definition works, too."

Laura waved both hands. "Hey, still here."

"Oh, we know, Ms. Watson. There's no way anyone could miss that." JT snorted with glee.

"Gee, try to do something nice for someone and this is what happens," Laura groused, which made both Seth and JT laugh.

"Yeah, you guys can come in." JT stepped aside. "I mean, Mom has a rule about no one in the house when she's not home, but I'm guessing that doesn't apply to cops and teachers."

Once inside, Laura's first impression was, wow. The house was beautifully furnished. Not quite the McMansion that JT had mentioned, but a well decorated home in a lovely neighborhood.

Laura wasn't sure what she expected, but her dislike for Mrs. Thomas might have colored her opinion of the type of house the woman would own.

JT led them into an immaculate living room. Curtains coordinated perfectly with the fabric on the furniture. Books were arranged artistically rather than functionally. Fresh flowers rested in an elegant vase on the coffee table.

JT seemed unsure of what to do next. "You wanna sit down, Ms. Watson? You look beat."

"I am beat. Thanks."

She sat on the couch, and Seth sat next to her. Now that JT was more at ease, Laura decided to broach her concerns. "JT, I stopped in because I was worried about you."

Guilt was written on the teen's face. "I'm fine. I felt a bit funky this morning, but I feel better now."

"So, you will be in school tomorrow?" Laura asked. "You're sure?"

Gone was the guilt and in its place was defiance. "Yeah. I wouldn't want to miss my detention."

"That's not why I was worried, and I think you know it," Laura said softly.

JT sighed, sounding much older than she looked. "Yeah, I do. None of my other teachers minded I was absent, I bet. Especially not Mrs. Lutz. She's the reason I'm serving detention."

Laura cocked her head to one side and raised her eyebrow. She'd found it was an effective expression when dealing with students. "She made you *not* turn in your homework?"

"No, but..."

Laura continued to stare at JT.

"No. But she didn't mind handing out the detentions. Mrs. Lutz hates me."

"Maybe that's not hate. Maybe it's frustration. Teachers feel frustrated when they can't reach a student. She wants you to excel. So do I."

"I don't know about Mrs. Lutz. I think what she really wants is for me to hurry up and finish her class so she can pass me on to some other teacher," JT replied, skepticism thick in her tone.

"And you think I'm here passing the buck, too?"

"No. You don't want me to do more detentions and brought my homework. Thanks."

Laura nodded. "That's part of it." She found herself adding, "And I was hoping if you caught up on your schoolwork tonight, you'd have time to come over and start that mural in the baby's room this weekend."

JT jumped and clapped. "You mean it?"

Laura hadn't intended to make the offer, but seeing JT's excitement, she was glad she had. "I told you it was a great design. And I don't mind being around the paints at school because we've got a great ventilation system, but at home, my only ventilation would be an open window. It's too cold for that, and I'd rather not be around the fumes long enough to paint the room myself, so you'll be doing me a huge favor."

It was more than paint fumes and Laura knew it. She wanted to be excited about this baby, but she couldn't manage it. And she needed to get things done. Her pregnancy was close to term. "Really, you'll be helping me out in a big way."

"Oh, man, this is so cool. I've got to pick up some paint and I can be at your house first thing Saturday morning."

"Why don't you make me a list of the supplies you want and I'll get those. And you'll need your mom's written permission." And to be on the safe side, Laura would make sure the principal knew JT was coming over to do the project. Teachers had to be very careful about socializing with students. There were lines you couldn't cross. "Spending time working on the actual mural is more than you should have to do as it is. I appreciate the favor."

"Ms. Watson, this isn't me doing you a favor, it's you doing me one. I wanted to paint a mural in my room, but my mom and her decorator nixed that idea. Of course, I wasn't planning on princesses. I outgrew that kid stuff a long time ago."

JT chuckled, but Laura thought it was a shame JT didn't believe in magic. Laura had found magic the day she'd found Jay. Her magic had died with him, too, but she wished JT could have believed longer. "Well, you can paint at my house till your heart's content, but the deal is, you do your homework tonight and catch up."

"Okay, you bet." JT stopped and stared at Seth. "You didn't say anything at all."

He shot them both a reassuring look. "I have sisters and I've learned that when women start talking a wise man gets quiet, unless he has something important to say, and even then, he should be quiet until they stop to breathe."

"Ouch. This time he wasn't picking on only me, he was picking on our entire gender." Laura smiled when JT laughed. Without her normal black outfit and outlandish makeup, JT seemed like a girl. Maybe Laura couldn't solve her student's problems, but she could give her this— a bit of happiness.

Laura stood. Well, that was a generous description. More accurately, she *tried* to stand. Her current girth made rising from couches less easy than chairs.

Seth sprang to his feet and offered her a hand.

She took it. "I've decided to forgive your gender-bashing given your chivalry."

Seth winked at JT. "See, Mom was right— show a lady some courtesy and you can get away with almost anything."

Laura mocked slugged his arm. "Maybe I take it back."

"You two sound like kids," JT scolded, though she was still grinning and obviously delighted.

Seth suddenly grew serious. "We may sound like kids, but we're both adults who are worried about you, JT. Remember we're here. You can talk to either of us, anytime, about anything."

JT eyed the earnest lieutenant, then nodded. "That's nice, but I'm fine. See you tomorrow, Ms.

Watson." She walked them to the front door. "Bye," JT said before she shut the door.

Laura looked at the door. "I hope that helped."

Seth nodded. "I think she knows you care. Sometimes that alone can make all the difference. Believe me, kids know when they're totally on their own, and it hurts."

Laura wanted to ask what he meant, but Seth's expression said he already regretted what he'd said. Hurriedly he added, "Maybe having at least one teacher believe in her will be enough."

"And maybe having a cop believe in her helps, too. I wonder about her mother, though. She doesn't seem to be around much." Laura shook her head. "How could any mother leave a child on their own so much?"

She thought about magic, her baby, and how she'd lost Jay, but still had this piece of him. Yes, that was magic.

Suddenly, she felt excited about painting the baby's room this weekend.

No matter what—this baby was her family.

"As for Saturday, could you use another hand?"

Laura looked at the tall cop. "Pardon?"

"I thought maybe I'd come help JT on Saturday, if you don't mind."

"No, I guess I don't, but—" They reached the truck and Seth got the door for her.

"Oh." Laura had never had a man hold a door for her before. Jay hadn't done it, and she'd never expected him to. She was sure Seth was doing it simply because she was pregnant and needed help to climb into his monster of a truck.

"You're a good man, Charlie Brown," she said as she got in the car.

SETH SAW LAURA'S SURPRISE. He might have blamed his mother for his good manners, but in reality, he didn't mind doing things like opening doors for women, although he was generally of the opinion that women were just as capable as men. But Laura had to be almost as wide as she was tall. Okay, that was an exaggeration, but still, she'd have been hard-pressed to climb in the truck without assistance.

Moments later he was behind the steering wheel. "I hope I didn't step on your toes, since some women take offense at a guy getting the door and..."

"My mother said, don't take offense where no offense was intended." Laura caught herself. "Well, she would have said that if she'd lived long enough to have those kind of talks with me." She felt embarrassed. "I was nine when she died, and that was too young for conversations like that. But in my head, she gave me all kinds of sage advice as I grew older. I mean, I knew she wasn't really there, but I felt better pretending, and most of her advice centered on being kind, so I figured it was all good."

"That's a shame, you losing your mom."

"Hey, Dad was great. We made a solid team."

Seth thought about it...he understood loss, but not to that extent. What Laura had gone through losing both her parents and a fiancé. Seth didn't say anything more on the subject as he drove toward the high school.

"How about you?" she finally asked. "You told me you have five siblings, but how about your parents. Are you close?"

"We were once, but not anymore."

"I'm sorry," Laura said softly.

For the first time since Allie died he admitted, "I am, too."

"Is there any way to fix things?"

He didn't answer. Couldn't. "So, about Saturday?"

Laura was kind enough to let him change the subject. "Sure. I have a little less than a month until Bbog is born—"

"Bog?" he asked.

"Bbog. Two B's. The night we found out we were pregnant, we referred to the baby as Baby-boy-or-girl. The next day, Jay sent me flowers and that was too long to fit on the florist's card, so he abbreviated it to Bbog and after that, well, that's how we referred to the baby."

"Bbog. It's original," he said diplomatically. "You haven't tried to find out what it is?"

"No. I want to be surprised. Jay wanted a girl, but I keep thinking it's a boy." She paused, then added, "About Saturday, thanks. I'd appreciate your help."

"Other than painting, what needs to be done?"

She sighed. "Everything."

"As in, put together the crib and set up the changing table everything?"

"Yes. I've tried, over and over again, but..."

Seth finished for her. "But you expected Jay to be there helping you, and it hurt too much to do it on your own." He got that. After Allie died, he'd had to take down everything they'd put together. It had bothered him so much, he'd sold the house and moved into his apartment.

He glanced over and saw Laura's shocked face.

"Yes, that's it. How did you know?"

"I was married once and my wife passed away." He couldn't bring himself to mention the babies he'd lost, as well. Not with Laura so close to delivering her own. So, he simply said, "I get it, Laura."

He'd felt a connection to her. A connection he hadn't felt with anyone else. Seth suspected that his checking on Laura didn't have much to do with the chief's request, or even JT. He and Laura both understood loss in a way few people did.

"Oh," she said slowly. "Oh, Seth, I'm sorry that you get it."

"Me, too. For both of us." Needing to lighten the mood, he said, "So, we'll make a party of it on Saturday? Enjoy ourselves...right?"

"Yes. That would be nice."

They drove the rest of the distance in companionable silence. Seth wished Laura would chatter about something, because otherwise he was left with thoughts of his parents and Allie.

His wife would be furious that he hadn't mended the rift with his parents. There were moments he so wanted to. He wanted to hug his mom, shake his dad's hand and assure them both that it was fine, that he forgave them. He simply hadn't been able to bring himself to say the words.

They'd wanted him to wait to marry Allie, saying that they were both too young. But if he'd listened and waited, he'd have missed so much. Maybe marrying right out of high school wasn't normally the wisest thing, but he treasured every one of those minutes with her.

After she'd died, his parents' words of sympathy had felt hollow. Every word of comfort they tried to offer, every gesture had set Seth's teeth on edge because all he could do was remember that they hadn't wanted him to marry her. He tamped down that old anger and concentrated on the here and now.

Since his brother Zac had gotten married, he'd been around his family more than he'd been in years. He'd made an uneasy truce with his parents for his brother's sake.

It wasn't the same relationship they'd once had, but it was *a* relationship. That would have to do.

CHAPTER THREE

LAURA LOVED HER SMALL house within walking distance to the school. When she'd bought it three years ago, she'd enjoyed decorating and arranging everything. It was perfect.

This room was not.

She stood at the door to what was once the guest room and now would be a nursery. Unfortunately, it didn't look like either at the moment. It looked like a storage room. A very disorganized storage room at that.

There were boxes and bags everywhere. For the last month she'd meant to come in and start sorting everything she'd bought for the baby's arrival, but every time she tried, she got as far as opening the door, then she'd simply shut it and back away.

It wasn't fair.

She was supposed to be doing this with Jay.

He was supposed to be here with her. They'd have called his parents, told them to come over and made a day of it. She'd have baked lasagna, and that crunchy garlic bread Jay liked so much. The aroma of it would have filled her small house and the sound of laughter would have filled every room as well.

They'd decided to live here for a few years and save money for something bigger. She always told Jay that the small size simply made the house more cozy. And on that day, it would have been cozy. Jay, his parents and her pregnant belly would have filled the house to the point of overflowing.

The thought of how it should have been hurt. It was a crippling pain that had the ability to take her breath away.

She put the pain aside, though, and concentrated on how it was now.

And how-it-was-now was that JT was going to paint a beautiful mural, and Seth was going to assemble the baby's furniture.

How-it-was-now, was that she was going to gather all the baby's clothes and wash them, then fold them and put them in drawers.

Laura forced herself into the room and pulled a bunch of Onesies out of a box. She'd ordered them from an online store. It's how she'd bought most of the baby's things. It seemed so much easier than traipsing to stores and having people ooh and aah over her ever-expanding stomach. Each time someone did that, she was hit anew with the thought that Jay should be there.

Stop.

She needed to stop thinking about Jay.

Which sounded so simple and was anything but.

She pulled out a Onesie. It had a picture of Einstein and the caption said *Brilliant Minds Have Bad Hair Days, Too*. She smiled. She could do this.

She marveled at how small the tiny sleepers were. Within weeks, Bbog would be wearing them as she held him or her.

She took off tags and filled the laundry basket with the baby's clothes, then struggled to her feet. She was so ready not to feel like a turtle who was stuck on his back, scrambling to find some way to right himself.

The doorbell rang.

Basket in hand, she opened the door to Seth.

He looked different out of uniform. Approachable.

Cute.

Thinking of Seth Keller as cute was disconcerting at best, downright disturbing at worst.

"Hey, what are you doing?" he asked by way of a greeting.

For a moment she worried that he knew she'd thought he was cute, but he came in, shut the door behind him and stared pointedly at the basket in her hand.

Laura felt a flood of relief. "Laundry? I mean, I'd have thought it was evident, but maybe not."

"You shouldn't be carrying anything." He took the basket from her hands.

"I can carry a basket of baby clothes. They weigh less than the grocery bags tend to."

"You shouldn't carry those eith—"

She was saved from another lecture and more disturbing thoughts about the man's cuteness when the doorbell rang.

Laura opened the door to find the once again scrubbed-looking JT wearing oversize denim overalls and a tight white shirt, carrying a small bag. Her mother was in the car and didn't look as if she was going to get out.

"Hi, Ms. Watson. Let's make some pretty pictures."

Seth put the basket down and went past them to JT's mother's car. He talked to her for a minute, then returned to the house. "I told her I'd take you home, if that was okay, and it was."

JT nodded. "Thanks. So, Ms. Watson, wanna show me the room?"

SETH LISTENED TO JT and Laura chatter away about painting techniques and the mural as he opened up the box that contained the crib. The instructions may as well have been in Greek.

Now, he was sure Greek was a fine language. He had friends who were Greek and Lori and Tony had a habit of calling each other Greek endearments, which he was sure Laura and JT would think was sweet. But he wanted his instructions in English. Not rocket scientist English, but rather plain old everyday English.

He examined the parts, assessing what he had and trying to picture what he had to do in order to turn them into a crib.

Laura left to start a load of baby clothes in the machine, and he said, "JT, look at this paragraph. See if it makes sense to you." He thrust the instructions at the girl.

She studied them for a moment and shrugged. "I don't get it."

"Could you read that paragraph while I try to follow along?"

JT studied the text, then shook her head. "No." She turned her back on him and started to sketch outlines on the wall.

He looked up and saw Laura standing in the doorway with a puzzled expression on her face as she stared at JT. "Why don't I help you?" she asked him. Laura read the instructions, step-by-step. And gradually, he made progress. She held a side as he screwed the headboard in place.

Forty-five minutes later, they had a crib.

"I'm gonna paint soon, Ms. Watson. You shouldn't be in the fumes."

"Okay. I'll make lunch." Seth jumped to his feet and offered her a hand. At first, he thought she wasn't going to take it, but good sense won out and she did. He got her to her feet and she headed into the hall.

Seth hung behind. "Can I do anything to help, JT?"

JT shook her head. "Nah. I like working on my own."

"I get that. But sometimes everybody needs a hand. Remember, I'm here. So's Ms. Watson. We're here to help with whatever you need."

JT turned toward him. "I know we're talking about more than helping with a mural. You're trying to be real sly and make sure I know that you two care. I sort of already figured it out. I don't know why. Why do you like me? I'm not the kind of kid most cops latch on to. And I can't figure out why Ms. Watson likes me. She's the only teacher at the school who does."

"That's not true."

JT snorted. "Yeah, it is. Of course, I'm a pain in the ass in class. I don't turn in homework and don't apply myself. I'm disruptive and according to one very helpful teacher, there's a chance I'm heading for a life of crime. She's got a whole list of things I do and don't do. Most of the time what I do do, I shouldn't. And what I don't do, I should. It's no way to endear yourself to the powers-that-be. I guess they have a reason not to really like me, which only makes it weirder that Ms. Watson seems to."

"So, why not apply yourself?"

"Why should I?"

Seth couldn't help but think of his mom. He knew exactly what she'd say if she were here. "My mom had this *option* speech. She'd say, you should always do your best in every class, no matter how much work it takes because each of those grades represents your future options. Maybe your future job won't depend on your grade in biology, but maybe you'll decide you want to be a doctor. Maybe you'll have this burning desire that eats at you—a feeling that your life won't be complete unless you become a doctor. Well, if you flunked out of your science classes, you won't have that option."

He'd heard the speech so many times growing up, it was like he was channeling Deborah Keller. "If she said that to me once, she said it a thousand times. For her, it wasn't about the grades, or the teachers, it was about me. About giving me the world. So, maybe you should give yourself as much of a chance as possible."

"Maybe I'm dumb enough that all the chances and all the trying in the world won't give me many choices, so what does it matter?"

Before he could come up with a response, JT pulled out some earbuds, stuck them in her ears and turned on an iPod, effectively tuning him out and his obviously unwanted advice.

He went back to the boxes and pulled out the pieces of a highchair. It was much easier to put together than the crib. Twenty minutes later, he carried it to the kitchen. "Where should this go?"

Laura smiled. "It's great, isn't it? How about we put it here." She gestured to the side of the table. "I normally use this chair, so it will be close. I bought a little cloth cushion for it. It's somewhere in all those boxes and bags."

"I'll find it. JT will holler at both of us if you try going into that room while she's painting." He paused. "She thinks she's dumb."

"Pardon?"

"I was talking to JT about leaving her options open by getting good grades, and it was easy to tell from her response that she doesn't think she could get good grades, even if she tried. So her philosophy seems to be, why bother?"

Laura chewed on her lip. "I'll talk to some of her other teachers next week. She still has detention with me. I'm pretty sure she'll be serving it until Thanksgiving, or after. I thought her teachers could tell me areas she needs help in and we could work on them while she's my captive."

Laura looked fierce. Determined to help JT, even if JT didn't want the help. She reminded him of Allie. His wife had gone into social work, filled with ideals, ready to save the world.

Seeing that same sense of commitment in Laura made him feel closer to her. "I hate to see any kid this lost. When they feel that it's hopeless...well, that's when we see them at the station. I don't want to find JT down there again."

Laura tore some lettuce and put it into a huge wooden bowl. "There's something about her, isn't there?"

"She reminds me of me," he admitted.

"Really?" She seemed surprised at the comparison.

Seth remembered what it felt like to think no one cared, to believe he had no future. "She's in pain. I'm no psychiatrist, and I don't know why, but I can see it. And I understand it, too. Every day since Allie died, I've hurt. It's like this gaping wound that scabs over, but the scab keeps getting ripped off. It's stupid things. Like holidays." Christmas was less than a month away. That was one of the most excruciating holidays. But all of them were hard.

"A certain song," Laura added. "The smell of his cologne as you walk through a store."

Seth nodded. "Going out on a starlit night...Allie loved the stars. She could name all kinds of constellations and would point them out to me and tell me their stories. I've never been able to see them like she could. When the scab comes off, it leaves me bleeding again. Makes me feel so alone. I see that in JT."

"Jay and I used to fight about the remote. Not really fight. It was one of those couple's mock-battles. We'd laugh as we jockeyed for control. Now, every time I pick it up, I wish he was here. I'd..."

She didn't need to finish the sentence because Seth got it. "Both of us understand pain and loneliness. Maybe that's why we're so drawn to JT and her problems."

"I hadn't thought of it that way." Laura looked thoughtful.

"I know why we hurt...we've both lost people we love. I'm not sure why she maybe feels this way. But I think when we figure that out, we'll be able to figure out how to reach her."

"So, we're allies?"

Seth liked the term. "That's a perfect way to describe us. Allies. For JT's sake."

"I'll talk to her teachers on Monday and maybe we'll have some clue."

"Maybe the school's counselor?" he suggested.

"I can give it a try." She paused. "Thanks for this." She waved her hands between them. "Defining us as allies. It makes me feel better."

He must have looked confused, because Laura continued, "I'll confess, I haven't let myself really think about it, but in the back of my mind, I thought maybe you were here because of Jay's dad."

"He's not the reason. He did ask me to let him know if you needed anything, but was actually very specific about not wanting me to feel like I was in the middle. He didn't want me spying on you. We're allies. He's my boss. They're two different and distinct relationships."

Laura seemed relieved. "Good. Thanks. You can tell him that I don't need anything from him or his wife. You can assure him of that."

Whatever was between the chief and Laura, it was clear that it ran deep. "Pain and anger. You, me and JT—the three of us seem to have it in spades. Hopefully, we'll figure out what caused JT's and help her get past it."

Was there hope for them, as well?

THE BABY'S ROOM WASN'T completely done, but, with Seth and JT's help, it was close. Laura went into school on Monday with some of her old optimism. She would find a way to help JT. She got a copy of JT's schedule in the office, and one-by-one, tracked down her teachers.

JT's science teacher handed her a stack of worksheets that JT could do for extra credit. JT's math teacher, while not offering up glowing comments did say that she did well with the pre-algebra questions in class, but she struggled with word problems.

Her French teacher said her spoken vocabulary was above average, but her written knowledge of the language was almost nonexistent and she gave Laura some flashcards to work with.

Laura found JT's English teacher at her desk during the her lunch break. She didn't know Debbie Lutz well. Debbie was older and had a different clique of teacher friends than Laura did, but they'd always been on good terms. She knocked softly on the open door to draw her colleague's attention. "Hey, Deb."

Debbie set her sandwich down and motioned Laura in. "Laura. Did you need something?"

Laura took the chair next to Debbie's desk, grateful to be off her feet. "I'm here to talk to you about JT Thomas."

Debbie grimaced. "What did she do now?"

"Nothing. She's serving detention with me and I wanted to get a feel for her schoolwork, and thought we could sort through a few of her problem areas."

"Well, I'm glad you only intend to work on a few of them, because if you intended to work on all of them, it would be a full-time job. The girl is one of the most uninspired students I've ever had—she's belligerent, insufferable, rude..."

Laura felt herself bristle at Debbie's obvious dislike of JT. "Fine. You don't like her. But my question is, what can I do to help her succeed in English?"

Debbie shrugged. "Nothing. She's hopeless."

"So, that's it? That's your teaching plan? Write her off before she's even reached the end of her first term of her freshman year?"

Debbie nodded. "Exactly. You're young and still idealistic, but take it from someone who's been teaching longer than you—sometimes there's nothing you can do for a student. Then the best thing to do is to cut them loose and concentrate on the students you can help."

Laura rose to her feet with more ease than she had in months. Her anger-induced adrenaline fueled her mobility. "I am not that young or that idealistic. Any idealism I once had died six months ago with my fiancé. And even now, at my most jaded, I would never write off a student. It's lazy, Debbie. If that's truly how you feel about teaching, maybe you should consider retiring before you do any further damage to the students."

Debbie stood as well and looked as if she was winding up for a response, but Laura didn't wait to hear it. She was too angry.

She stormed out of the room.

Her adrenaline, though, could only take her so far. Still, she made her way to the teacher's lounge and found a dark-haired stranger pouring herself a cup of coffee. "Bad day?" she asked.

"No," Laura snapped and realized this poor stranger had nothing to do with Debbie Lutz's lack of professionalism. "Sorry. It's actually been a productive day. Fine, even. The last few minutes, not so much."

Laura sank into a vacant chair and forced herself to take a deep breath and calm down.

The woman nodded and joined Laura at her table. "Trouble with a student?"

"Sort of. It led to talking to a particular teacher whose attitude was far more troubling." She extended a hand. "I'm Laura Watson."

"Eli Keller."

"Eli?" The name niggled at her. "Possibly related to Lieutenant Seth Keller? He mentioned an Eli."

"He's my brother-in-law. You know him? He mentioned me?"

Laura felt it was probably better for Seth if she didn't repeat his comment comparing his pregnant sister-in-law Eli to the equivalent of a house.

"He'd mentioned you'd had a baby." Laura patted her own huge stomach. There, that was diplomatic. "But he didn't say anything about you taking a job here."

"I'm not. I run the teen parenting program in Whedon. I'm here for a meeting with the other directors. They're in the next room talking. I'm supposed to be on a bathroom break, but stopped in for this." And she waved her cup. "I'm surprised that Seth even mentioned me at all." She shook her head as if realizing she was talking out of turn and changed the subject. "So, what teacher had you so annoyed?"

The fact that Eli didn't work here made Laura feel more comfortable asking advice from her. "I have a student, a freshman. She's been in nonstop trouble since September. I went to ask her English teacher about her and..." Remembering the conversation made Laura's blood boil. "She told me the girl's a lost cause and I should let it go. Well, I won't."

Eli frowned. "I work with pregnant girls and teen moms. If their parents, teachers and classmates think of them as lost causes, I won't. I'm there to help them stay in school, find whatever resources they need to make that happen. After they graduate, I try to encourage them to continue their education at colleges, or tech schools. That's our job. To teach. To prod. To do whatever it takes so our kids succeed. Never mind this teacher. Be there for your student. Be ready to lend an ear, a hug, or to kick butt if need be."

"I'm an art teacher."

"And once upon a time, I'd have been called a Home Ec teacher. Now I'm a Consumer and Family Science teacher. Doesn't matter what label they use. It's the teacher part that matters. No, I take that back. It's the heart part that matters. You care for this girl. That matters. If anything is going to reach her, that will."

Laura agreed. She liked this woman, Seth's sister-in-law. "I've been wondering about her reading." She felt more confident now that she'd said the words aloud. "Her math and French teachers both mentioned something about it."

"Frankly, I think the most direct approach is best. Ask her. Flat out. When I have a girl I suspect is in trouble, that's my approach. Head-on. I don't wait for them to come to me."

The advice made sense. "Thanks."

"Anytime. About Seth—how is he?" Eli quickly added, "We don't see much of him. I know Zac worries."

"He's good." Laura remembered his talk of scabs that never really heal. "He's helping me with this student."

"Friends?" Eli asked.

Laura thought about it. They'd defined themselves as allies, but friends worked, too. "Yes."

"Good. Everyone needs to feel as if they have someone in their corner." Eli got up and rooted around in her bag. "Here's my card. Call me if I can do anything for you, this student or for Seth."

"Thank you, so much."

"Anytime." Eli started toward the door, then stopped and turned around. "How exactly did my name come up in conversation?"

"Uh, he was reassuring me that I wasn't the biggest pregnant woman he'd ever seen."

Eli Keller started laughing. "No, you're not. I was huge. Big as a house."

"I think the term they used for me was McMansion."

Eli laughed even harder. "How long until you're due?"

"Only a few weeks left."

"Good luck. A baby changes everything. I can't believe my Johnny's two already."

If Eli Keller was any indication, Zac came from a nice family. Laura couldn't help but wonder what had happened with them and Seth. Why didn't they see much of him?

She got through the rest of the day and was determined to follow Eli Keller's advice and ask JT straight out if she had problems reading, but JT had a dentist appointment after school and only stopped in long enough to tell Laura she'd see her tomorrow and make up the missed detention.

Laura mulled over JT's circumstances, and was thankful when Seth called that night. He was working second shift, but he'd taken to checking in with her most evenings. She didn't want to admit that she looked forward to those conversations.

Discussing JT with Eli had been nice, but saying the words to Seth made her tension over the matter ease. "Both her French teacher and her math teacher mentioned problems with vocabulary. She's so smart, but what if she's having problems reading? That would explain why, despite her intelligence, she's floundering in school."

"That would explain her reaction when I asked for help with the crib instructions," he mused. "So what are you going to do?"

"I'm not an English teacher, and this isn't my specialty. I know more about teaching basket weaving than reading. But I talked to another teacher and—"

She was going to tell him about meeting Eli and her suggestion, but he interrupted. "Hey, sorry. I've got to go. We have a call."

"No problem. Bye."

She'd speak to him about Eli next time she saw him. What she wouldn't tell him was his sister-in-law's comments about his relationship with his family. His difficulties with them were his, as her difficulties were with hers.

They were allies, but they weren't close enough to go butting into each other's lives.

That's what she planned to tell him.

The baby kicked, and she chose to believe it was in agreement.

CHAPTER FOUR

THE NEXT DAY, LAURA was ready when JT came into her classroom to serve her detention. The girl was in all black, including a black pair of combat boots. She threw her books on a desk, but before she could sit down, Laura motioned her to the front of the room.

"What's up, Ms. Watson? Hey, I wanted to know if I could come do more work on the mural. I have this idea—"

Laura nodded at the chair next to the desk.

"Before we talk about the mural, JT, we have to talk about another topic."

The girl looked nervous. "Did I do something else?"

"No, nothing like that. It's..." Laura hesitated. Part of her wanted to ease into the subject, but instead, she jumped in head-first and handed JT a book. "I'd like you to read the first page to me."

JT glanced at the book, then at Laura. "Why?"

"Because I asked you to."

JT passed the book back to Laura. "Read it yourself."

"That's how you reacted the other day when the lieutenant asked you to read the instructions to him. And when I talked to your teachers—"

JT looked furious. "Why did you talk to them?"

"Because I'm worried about you. We're in your third month of high school, and you seem to be floundering. You're passing your classes, although not by much. Mostly D's and two very low C's. Your French teacher said she was very pleased with your spoken vocabulary, but your written vocabulary wasn't nearly as good. Your math teacher said you did great on equations, but had trouble with word problems. Do you see the theme? I do. So, JT, *do* you have difficulty reading?"

JT kicked the side of Laura's desk. Her heavy boot made a thud that reverberated. "I'm not stupid."

"No one said you were," Laura said gently. "But little things you've said and done lead me to believe you might be having a problem."

"Yeah? Well, if I'm so stupid and can't read, how'd I make it to the ninth grade?"

"If I had to guess, I'd say you're very smart and learned a bunch of tricks that have helped you get by. That maybe when you're asked to read something you don't feel comfortable with, you get mad and cop an attitude." She pointed at the book on her desk. "Anger is a great way of deflecting a problem."

"First, you're a reading expert, now, you're a psychiatrist? Gee, it must be nice to know it all, Ms. Watson."

"Being snarky might work with other people, but I'm not backing down, JT."

"You talked about my math and French teachers, but how about my English teacher? I bet Ms. Lutz didn't tell you I had a reading problem. Bet she said I was a waste of time."

Laura didn't respond because although Debbie hadn't used those exact words, in essence that's what she'd said.

"How come none of my English teachers ever said something? None of 'em, ever."

"I don't know. But I'm saying something. I noticed. And I'm not going to let you pretend this away."

JT glared at Laura. "I can read fine."

Laura handed the book back to her. "Then read the first page."

JT shook her head. "I don't have to prove anything to you. I don't owe you anything."

"No, you don't have to prove anything to me, and you certainly don't owe me anything, but I'm not going to stop nagging until you read a page out loud to me."

"Why do you care?" JT burst out and jumped to her feet. "I've been trying to figure it out and can't. Are you some do-gooder, or are you trying to find something to do since your baby's daddy died? I'm not some distraction for you." She paced to and fro in front of Laura's desk.

JT's remark had been a direct hit, but Laura wouldn't let her own pain dissuade her from what needed to be done. "JT, nothing, and no one could distract me from the pain of losing my fiancé. You're not some charity case, some cause for me to focus on. This is me, caring about you. This is a teacher who's concerned about a student. Read the page." She picked up the book and held it out to JT, waiting.

"No."

Laura had found that sometimes the best argument was saying nothing. She simply continued holding the book and staring at JT, waiting.

JT's pacing slowed, and she glanced at Laura and the book, but didn't say anything, either.

The minutes ticked by. Normally, Laura liked the sound of the clock. Each tick meant she was that much closer to the end of a school day, and when she was in a very pregnant mood, it was a reminder she was that much closer to her baby's arrival. But today, those ticks represented a contest of wills. Hers against JT's. And this was one battle Laura intended to win.

Five minutes must have passed and Laura was ready to set the book down. Her arm was starting to shake from the effort of holding it, when JT sat back in the chair and took the book from her.

She opened it to the first page. "The. WI. N. D. OW. Was. OP. OP. Op. En."

She slammed the book shut. "There. I read it. I can read, so you can quit worrying."

"JT, you read a sentence. Painfully. Laboriously."

"But I read it."

Laura was by no means an expert when it came to teaching reading, but she knew there was a difference between being able to push your way through the letters and words, and being able to read.

"Listen, JT, I'm an art teacher, but even I know that being able to read easily is necessary in life. I want that for you. You'd have so much less trouble with your classes. Mr. Fritz, the guidance counselor, can set up some special—"

"No." JT stood again. "He's not gonna put me in the stupid classes. I won't go. I'll quit school first."

"JT, sit down. I'm trying to help."

Laura wasn't sure JT would listen, but after a moment, she took her seat again.

She hit the desk with her fist. "You want to help by putting me in with the rejects?"

"That's not kind, and it's beneath you. They're simply students who have problems, or who need help to learn more efficiently. You need some extra help in order to—"

"If you put me in that class, I'm out of here. I mean it, I'll quit school."

"JT." Laura didn't know what to say. She didn't know how to communicate with this girl. She knew in her heart that helping JT wasn't some way to fill the void. Laura was a teacher, trying to do her job. More than that, she liked the girl.

"Fine. I love reading, but I'm no English teacher. Still, if you let me, I'll help you."

Her offer seemed to surprise JT. "Huh?"

"I'll help you. I'll pick up some material, and then you and I will work here after school each day."

"You're not going to turn me in?"

Laura shook her head. "I was never going to *turn you in.* I am going to talk to the principal—"

"No reject classes, right?"

"Right. You'll have to promise to work hard. But working hard to learn to read better can't be any more difficult than struggling with words and having to cover it up."

JT didn't have an outburst this time. She didn't look angry or frustrated. She looked truly confused. "Why? You never answered why?"

Laura smiled. "I like you. Why is that so hard to believe?"

JT shrugged. "I do look in the mirror, so, I know, most people see the piercings and all the black."

"I am not most people. And you really need to see that you are special. You're worth caring about."

JT snorted her response.

"May I talk to Seth, too? He noticed and is worried."

"Yeah, but that's it. No one else." She paused. "He's gonna think I'm dumb."

"No, he won't."

"You know, you're kind of naive, Ms. Watson."

"And you know, you have a great vocabulary. I'm not sure what to do to help, but we'll figure it out between us. For now, why don't you go get your books and begin your homework. Wouldn't it be novel if you went in tomorrow with it all done?"

"My teachers would probably faint from shock. Especially Mrs. Lutz. She hates me."

"Let's not worry about what the teachers or anyone else says or thinks. Let's worry about you."

THAT SAME NIGHT, SETH walked into his spartan apartment. Normally, he wouldn't have noticed. But his sisters, May, Layla and Cessy had come to Erie to shop a few weekends ago and had stopped by to take him to dinner. His youngest sister, Cessy, never one to mince words, had summed up their collective opinion. "Seth, I've seen prison cells that look better than this place."

Her comment had stuck with him ever since.

He had a desk with a laptop on it and a sectional in the main room. The small kitchenette off to the right was more than adequate for the amount of cooking he did, and he didn't need more than the stool and the counter for the infrequent times he actually ate at home.

The bedroom to the left of the main room had a king-size bed and a dresser.

It was functional.

And Cessy was wrong because he didn't know of any prison cell with a sixty-inch flat-screen television. He'd been saying as much to himself for the last week—it wasn't helping. He still noticed how bare his apartment seemed, but he didn't know what to do about it.

His place with Allie had been warmer and felt like a home. His parents and Laura had managed it, too. It wasn't just that they had more stuff. It was a feeling. And while he could go buy more things to put in his apartment, he couldn't buy that feeling.

He gave up staring at the empty apartment and looked up *illiteracy* on Google.

Then he narrowed the search and added *high school.*

For the next hour he surfed the net, then left for Borders and picked up two of the books the most helpful website had suggested. Afterward, he headed to Laura's.

Her house was small, and painted a deep gray. It was in a quiet neighborhood not far from his apartment. The place had red shutters, and a small porch bordered by holly bushes, which were still green, despite the November cold.

He knocked on the cherry-red door. He wondered if she'd bought the car to match the door, or vice versa.

Laura opened it as far as the chain would allow, then closed it. He heard the rattle as she took the chain lock off, then reopened the door, this time with worry on her face. "Seth? Is something wrong with JT? Is she back in jail?"

"She was never in jail," he assured her. "But no, nothing like that. You said you know basket weaving not teaching reading, wasn't that it?" He held the books out to her.

She smiled and nodded. "Come in."

He liked that phrase a lot. And as he stepped into Laura's hallway, he was struck by how non-spartan her home seemed. It was warm and inviting. There was a coat tree standing next to the door. A long, skinny table next to it. It had a small bowl with keys in it, and a trimmed ivy plant.

Maybe a plant would make his sisters feel better about his house?

"Seth?"

"Sorry." He stopped worrying about his unadorned apartment and concentrated on JT. "Anyway, did you know that about a fifth of high school seniors can be considered functionally illiterate? A website suggested these books. They're easy readers for older students. I thought they'd be good for JT."

"This way," Laura said.

He went back into the small, but neat house. Growing up, his parents' house had been controlled chaos, and his place seemed sterile. Laura's house was a vision of neatness and order. But despite those differences, it said *home* here as much as his parents' had. As much as his apartment didn't.

Wow, Cessy's comment had bothered him even more than he thought.

"I was making some soup for dinner. Would you like a bowl?" Laura asked.

"You don't have to feed me."

"My grandmother used to say, *I don't have to do anything but die and pay taxes.*" Laura stopped abruptly as she said the words. "I guess that's the truth of it. Things happen. And the people left behind have to go on. That seems the hardest part."

"I never thought of it that way," Seth said as he pulled a stool up to the island.

Laura bustled around at the stove, not looking at him as she said, "Well, I know that Jay's fine. I know he'd want me to find a way to be happy. Although, I'm not sure how to do it."

"It hasn't been that long for you," Seth said softly. He remembered those awful early days and acknowledged how far he'd come. He'd healed without even noticing it. He missed Allie. He always would. But he'd survived. He'd found a life for himself.

He'd told Laura that Allie's death was like a scab that kept getting torn off, but he confessed it had been a long time since he'd dealt with that particular scab. He wasn't sure if he found that idea comforting.

Laura was staring at him. "And you? How long for you?"

"Years." He could no longer automatically say how long to the day. He did the math in his head. "It's going on three years. I still feel the loss, but it's not that giant, clawing grief."

"So, my goal should be to get out of this hole and..." She shrugged. "And then what?"

"And then, once you can see beyond that hole, you'll be able to see your future. You'll be able to remember there's so much more to life and you'll want to be a part of it."

She dished up bowls of soup. "You haven't."

"Haven't what?"

She set a bowl in front of him. "Moved past your loss."

"Most days I have. And that's something."

She sat down opposite him at the island, her own bowl in front of her. "Maybe it is." She stirred her soup with her spoon, not taking a bite.

He took a taste. "Hey, this is good."

"Thanks." She continued to stir. Round and round. Finally, she said, "So, about JT—"

Seth prided himself on reading people, but he had no clue what the expression on Laura's face meant. "Laura?" he asked.

She stood up, looked at the floor, then panicked. "I think my water broke!"

"Oh." The realization sunk in. "Oh! Come on, I'll take you to the hospital."

"No, really, that's okay. I gotta get some dry pants, and my suitcase. I'll drive myself. I'll need a car to get home," she said, as if that explained everything.

"Who should I call?"

Sadness replaced the panic.

"A friend?" he asked.

"This was supposed to be me and Jay. Having someone else come along..." She shook her head and her long, blond hair flew back and forth. "I can't do it."

"What about the chief and his wife?" Seth knew without a doubt that Jameson and his wife would be at the hospital in a heartbeat.

"No!" Laura couldn't have been more emphatic. There was only one option left, but Seth didn't want to take it. He wished he was the kind of man who could say, *Fine, good luck,* and go home, but he wasn't. "I'll drive you then," he insisted.

"No. I need my car—"

"Damn it, Laura, I'll pick you up when it's time to go home. You don't need a car."

"I need to do this on my own." Her voice sounded suspiciously watery.

"Are you crying?" he asked this woman for a second time.

"No, I'm not crying. And I don't need you. I need to do this by myself."

"No, you don't." He reached for her hand.

She pulled her hand away. "You don't understand."

"So explain it to me."

"My water broke and you want to do an in-depth psychological assessment of me?" She no longer sounded panicked or as if she were going to cry.

"Laura, I'm not going anywhere except with you to the hospital, so like I said, you might as well explain it to me. I want to help."

"But we've both learned that what you want isn't always what you get. Now, if you don't mind..."

Seth wasn't biting. "I do mind."

"You're a pain in my butt, Keller." There was no heat in her accusation.

Despite the fact he was scared to death that he was arguing with a woman in labor, he managed a halfhearted chuckle. "You are definitely not the first person to tell me that. I had three sisters who never used to put it that politely. And my brothers were even more graphic and free with their descriptions."

"You're not going to go until I tell you something."

"Not only something, the truth." What he didn't say was that he wasn't going anywhere even after she explained herself.

"Fine. How's this for the truth? I was supposed to say, 'Honey, my water broke,' and have Jay run around the house like a madman because he was so nervous, even though he was trying to be tough-guy cop cool. He'd speed trying to get me to the hospital and I'd laugh and say one of his buddies was going to ticket him if he didn't slow down. And when I was in labor, in the middle of a bad contraction, I'd look at him and he'd be suffering for me, and I'd know how it hurt him to think I was in pain, so I'd try to be stoic for his sake."

She definitely was crying. Seth grabbed a napkin and handed it to her.

Laura wiped her eyes and continued. "And when I gave birth, he'd hold our baby first and he'd have tears in his eyes, knowing that the two of us brought this tiny being into this world because of our love."

She wiped her eyes again. "Don't you see, Seth? I've had this baby with him in my dreams and fantasies a thousand times since we found out I was pregnant. Even after he died, I couldn't stop imaging how it *should* be. Even though it won't happen that way. And the truth is—the utter truth of it is—if I can't have that, I don't want anything or anyone else there with me because there is no substitute. I'll be raising this baby on my own, and that seems ever so much harder than giving birth on my own."

Seth wanted to reach out and hold her more than he'd ever wanted to do anything, but he knew she wouldn't allow it. That she couldn't allow it. She needed to feel in control. She needed to feel confident that she could do this on her own. And he, more than most, could understand.

So he simply said, "Let's compromise. You go change and get your stuff, and let me drive you."

She tried to look disgruntled, but the napkin she was using to blot her eyes ruined the effect. "That's not a compromise." She sniffed. "That's you getting your own way."

"Like I said, three sisters. I learned at an early age how to cope with girls."

"I—" He thought she was going to tell him no, or yell about his use of the word *girl,* but she simply shook her head in exasperation, much like his sisters used to, and said grudgingly, "Fine. You can drive me, but then you have to go."

He didn't agree, and didn't disagree. He shooed her toward her room. "Change."

Laura muttered her way down the hall. She gave up on muttering and was silent on the ride to the hospital.

Seth tried to think of something to say, but kept drawing a blank. Eventually, he hit on, "Should I call JT and tell her that you're having the baby so that she doesn't think you deserted her tomorrow at detention?"

"Yes. I thought I had more time before the baby."

"You'll be on maternity leave for a while?"

"Yes. At least three months. I may just take the rest of the school year. It would be unpaid, but I have enough put away." She was quiet then.

Things were a blur when they got to the hospital. They whisked Laura away to get her ready. Seth had no idea what that entailed, and he didn't ask. He didn't know what to do. He couldn't leave her, but he didn't want to be here. He was a casual acquaintance, an ally at best.

He thought again of calling the chief. He was stuck between a rock and a hard place here. On the heels of that thought, a nurse said, "Your wife is all settled in the birthing room."

"She's not my wife."

The tiny woman in scrubs and a ponytail frowned. "Your girlfriend, then."

"No, we're not—"

She interrupted him, frustration in her voice. "Your baby-mama, then. She's settled and you can go in."

The room the nurse showed him into didn't look like an ordinary hospital room. Pictures of babies were on the walls. And there was a rocking chair and recliner. "Nice room," he said, for lack of anything else.

"The nurse said you were still here. Really, you can go now. But thanks for driving me. I guess it would have been dangerous if I'd had a huge labor pain in the middle of traffic."

"Any yet?"

"No. Not yet. The nurse said normally they start within twenty-four hours after your water breaks. She would have let me go home, but says I shouldn't be alone, so I'm here for the duration.

It's a waiting game now. If I'm not in labor by the morning, they'll probably induce me."

He pulled the rocking chair next to the bed. "Well, it looks like we're in for a long night. Why don't you see if there's anything on television?" He plunked down in the chair like Custer making his last stand, and like Custer, he had a feeling this wasn't going to end well.

"Seth, really. Go home."

"Hey, I'm not staying for the messy bits, but I'm also not leaving you alone to wait. So, we'll wait together. Watch some TV. Maybe I'll visit the gift shop before it closes and see if there's a deck of cards I can buy."

"Seth…"

"Laura, it's no use arguing. Unless you call someone else, I'm staying."

"Fine. I challenge you to Five Hundred Rummy. And I should warn you, I'm quite the card shark."

CHAPTER FIVE

LAURA STUDIED SETH AS HE slept in the recliner. His features had eased and he looked much younger. She tried to guess how old he was. Maybe late twenties? Certainly not more than thirty, tops. She wondered how his hair would grow in if it wasn't so short. Would it be straight, or would it curl if he let it get long? She couldn't imagine him letting it get too long. He was too much a cop for that. This shorter cut suited him without making him look forbidding. He looked...safe. Like someone you could trust.

She was wondering why he was here and what she was going to do with him, when the first contraction hit. She'd read the books and gone to class and she expected the first contraction to be more of a cramping than anything else.

This wasn't that.

It wasn't some gentle introduction to the world of contractions. It was so fierce it took her breath away.

Ten minutes later, another came.

By one o'clock, she called in a nurse who woke up Seth to kick him out of the room so the nurse could check her progress.

The nurse declared Laura was at five centimeters and went to update the doctor.

"This next stage goes faster and the contractions come quicker and will get more intense," she warned Laura.

More intense? Laura groaned.

"Is it safe yet?" Seth called from the doorway.

"For now," she told him. "But I think this is the part you were talking about. The—what was it? Messy bits? I think this is that, so it's time for you to go."

"Maybe I'll stay a while longer. I can help you with your breathing." He hee-hooed at her.

"How do you know about that?"

"My wife..." He hesitated, took a deep breath and continued, slowly. "She was pregnant when she died. We'd only taken a few classes, but after sitting on a floor and panting with total strangers for an hour, the lessons sort of stick."

His wife had been pregnant? And he was here with her? Laura felt an overwhelming urge to cry, but knew Seth wouldn't welcome that. "Oh, Seth."

"Before, when you were talking about having this baby in your fantasies, I used to do the same thing. Imagine I was with Allie having our twins. I helped her breathe. She would get tired and cranky and yell at me, but I didn't mind.

And when she had the first baby, I held it while she delivered the second. I imagined it over and over, Laura. And I also know, no one should do this alone."

Twins? He'd lost three people when Allie died. Twins and a wife.

She felt humbled by his strength, because she wasn't sure she'd have survived something like that. It made her more resolved than ever to do this on her own. But more importantly, Seth shouldn't—couldn't—stay now that she knew. "You're wrong. I need to do this on my own, so you—" Another contraction hit before she could tell him to leave, and as if the nurse was some sort of seer, this one was the worst yet. Laura held her breath and tried to keep from crying out.

"No, don't do that." Seth grabbed her hand and got right up in her face, forcing her attention to center on him. "Breathe, Laura. In. Out. Look at me, Laura, and breathe."

Time lost all sense of meaning to Laura. The idea of fighting with Seth or forcing him to do anything was long since forgotten. Laura's world narrowed to contractions and the minutes in between, which were fewer and fewer.

And there was Seth. Breathing with her. Feeding her ice chips.

She wanted to be annoyed at his heavy-handed decision to stay, but secretly she was grateful. This would have been so much harder without him here.

He was putting himself through hell to help her. During the moments of rational thought, she knew that.

But rational thought was in short supply. All she could do was remember to breathe and ride out one contraction after another.

At some point the nurse came back in. Laura was about to ask Seth to leave so the nurse could check her progress, but another contraction hit, and Seth was staring into her eyes, making her focus on him. "Breathe," he commanded. As the contraction ebbed, the nurse's hand was beneath the sheet and she did a discreet check.

"You're almost there," she said with a bright perkiness that made Laura want to scream.

"She's so darned cheerful," she muttered to Seth.

He was sitting next to her on the edge of the bed, holding her hand, and chanting, "Look at me, Laura. Breathe. Breathe."

At some point the doctor and nurse returned to them. In the few seconds between contractions, the doctor checked her and declared, "You're totally effaced, Laura. You'll feel the urge to push soon."

He positioned Seth behind her on the bed, so she could lean against him. She should have protested. She would have protested if she had the energy. She waited for him to say, *Gotta go now*, but all he did was listen to the doctor's instructions, and let her rest against his chest.

He felt warm and solid. As if he'd never let anything happen to her or this baby.

And though Laura had given up believing in that kind of surety, for now, it was comforting as she began to push.

Laura had thought the contractions were bad, but this was a whole new level of pain. And yet, she forgot to be embarrassed that Seth was here. She simply pressed against him during the minuscule breaks and appreciated his strength.

She didn't worry about should-have-beens.

About her future as a single mother.

All she could do was concentrate on the next pain.

The next push.

The brief respite.

Then the cycle starting again.

Finally, the doctor said, "Don't push, just breathe a moment."

She fought against her body's need to push.

Seth stroked her hair. He murmured things in her ear, telling her she was amazing, that she could do this, that he was here for her.

His touch and his words helped.

"Okay, Laura," the doctor said, "we're almost there. This next contraction—"

She lost the doctor's words as the next contraction hit and she pushed.

And suddenly, the urge evaporated and there was a huge feeling of relief from the pressure.

"It's a boy," the doctor announced.

"A boy?" She was trying to digest the fact that she had a son, when Seth hooted. "You did it, Laura. You were fantastic and you did it. You've got a boy. A son!"

And as the nurse handed her a baby, the reality sank in. She had a son.

Laura felt a rush of love like nothing she'd ever felt before. Her love for this tiny boy was so immense it overwhelmed her. Every doubt, every insecurity. All the pain. There was just her, leaning against Seth, holding her baby.

He reached around her and gently touched the baby's cheek with the back side of his index finger. "He's beautiful, Laura."

For a moment, it was as if the three of them were the only people in the room. The doctor did whatever he was doing and the nurse helped, but it was all lost on Laura as she stared into her son's eyes. He was awake and not crying. He stared at her, as if he was as amazed at this turn of events as she was.

"It's all right," she crooned to him. And she knew with a bone-deep sense of surety, that it was. She immediately looked at Seth. He should have been in a room like this with his wife; she should have been here with Jay. And yet, here they were. Together they'd brought her son into the world. What could you say to a man who would do that?

"Thank you," she finally managed, though it seemed inadequate.

Seth seemed uncomfortable. "I should probably go and let the doctor finish...things." He hurried out of the room, as if suddenly realizing where he was.

Laura missed his steady presence and felt guilty that she did. She couldn't afford to rely on Seth. She couldn't rely on anyone. It was just her and the baby.

She stared at her son. Nothing about his birth was the way she'd planned, but he was here now. He was hers. She wouldn't let him down. He could rely on her, she silently promised the baby, and herself.

After they'd cleaned her up and the baby, the doctor and nurse left, and Seth came back into the room.

He walked over to her and she took his hand. "I know I said I could do this on my own, but I don't think I could have. Thank you."

With his free hand, he smoothed a strand of hair from her cheek. "Laura, if I've learned nothing else tonight, I've learned that you can do anything. That was..." He was silent, as if searching for the right word. "Amazing. No, a miracle. I've heard them talk about the miracle of childbirth, but I never understood it until tonight. Thank you for that."

She felt suspiciously close to tears.

"Would you like to hold him?"

BEFORE HE COULD SAY NO, Seth held the baby in his arms. He intended to hand him back right away, but the baby looked at him. That's all it took. That one little wide-eyed look captivated him. He seemed so small. So tiny. And Seth felt such a strong need to protect him. To keep this one little scrap of humanity away from harm.

"What's his name?" His own voice sounded alien to his ears. Husky with pent-up emotion.

"Jameson Alexander Martin, III. After his father, not his grandfather," she added quickly.

"Jameson Alexander Martin, III." He laughed. "That's quite a mouthful for a little guy."

"I'm going to call him Jamie."

"Jamie Martin. I like that." He studied the baby, and he could almost imagine Jamie was his. That he and Allie had been through the last grueling hours together, and were now here with their babies. But the moment passed, and Seth knew that fantasy was over. He wouldn't need to recall it. He'd experienced it with Laura. He should have thanked her for sharing the experience with him. It was more surprising and more intense than he'd ever imagined.

He felt a pang of guilt. This should have been something he'd shared with Allie. He pushed away the thought and concentrated on what was. The baby in his arms was here and real, and he'd had a part in that—a small part. Reluctantly, he handed Jamie back to his mother. "I should go now and let the two of you get some rest."

"Seth, you do realize it's Wednesday?" Laura sounded worried.

"Yes."

"'Wednesday's child is full of woe.' That's how that old poem goes. He's already lost his dad. That's more than enough woe for any baby, don't you think?" Tears filled her eyes.

"I'm not Jay, Laura. I'd never try to be him. But I'm here for Jamie. Not just now, tonight. Long-term. He can count on me. And before you ask, this has nothing to do with the chief, or anything else. This has to do with this little boy. I was here for his birth, and I choose to believe I'm meant to be a part of his life. So, he won't know woe. He'll know the safety and security of a mother who loves him and a—" he paused, fighting for the right word "—a friend who will always be here for him."

She sniffled. "Thanks. It must be the hormones. As much as pregnancy sends them out of whack, giving birth is worse."

"Hormones and exhaustion. That was some of the hardest work I've ever seen anyone go through. You need sleep. I'll be back tomorrow, or rather, later today."

"Thank you again for everything. Of course, this will teach you to be a nice guy."

"Pardon?"

She tucked the baby's blanket around a foot that had escaped. "I mean you stopped in to drop off some books and tell me about your research, like the nice guy you are, and look what happened."

"I got lucky. Thank you for sharing this with me." He leaned down and kissed her cheek. "Now, get some rest. I'll check in on you both later."

SETH HAD NEVER BEEN so tired and yet so exhilarated in his life.

He paused, considering whether or not he should do it. "Hello?"

Seth recognized his mother's voice. "Hi, Mom."

"Seth?" His mother sounded surprised, and tentative.

"It's me."

"Is something wrong?"

He hated to admit it, but even if he had a problem, he wouldn't call home. He hadn't called to chat since he graduated from high school and married Allie. He'd never cut them totally off. He saw them, but he kept them at arm's length.

"No, nothing. I..." He paused, searching for an excuse. "I wanted to see if Cessy was home. When she came over the other day, she asked if I wanted to go help her buy some new skis and I'm off next Saturday."

"Oh. Seth, she's sleeping."

He glanced at the clock. "Jeez, Mom, I'm so sorry. I didn't realize it was four in the morning. My sense of time is messed up."

"Seth, you can call me anytime, day or night. And you know me, early in the morning is my favorite time of day."

"It was the only time the house was quiet." Six kids. How had his parents managed?

"Well, you weren't an overly quiet lot." She paused and asked, "How are you?"

Part of him wanted to tell her about his night, about Laura. He wanted to talk about how much Jamie's birth had meant to him. He wanted to tell her about the joy he'd felt as he'd held the baby, and the guilt he'd felt at it not being Allie wth him. His mom would help him sort out his feelings. He needed to talk about it, but it had been so long since he'd had a meaningful conversation with either of his parents that he simply countered by asking, "How is everything there?"

He could hear his mother's sigh over the phone. It was soft. So soft, a stranger would never have noticed, but despite their rift, he wasn't a stranger and he knew he'd hurt her again by not answering. She let that slide, however, and said, "Fine. Everything here is fine. Dom came for dinner this weekend. He got a job in Pittsburgh working for the VA." Seth's younger brother, Dominick had graduated with a degree in physical therapy and had talked about working with veterans. Because of his leg braces, he'd never be able to serve in the military, but he said by working with vets he'd be doing his part.

"Good for him. I'll call him. Any other news?"

"Layla's still working at the cancer center." Layla lived in Pittsburgh, too. She went down there to Carlow University because Dom was in Pittsburgh, and like him, she'd stayed.

"And May?" he asked. May would have driven most parents crazy. She moved from job to job, from town to town, always looking for something, and never finding it.

He could hear his mother's smile. "She's a barista this week and thinking about writing the next great American novel."

May was continually finding herself. Each new discovery meant a new job and frequently a new city. She'd been in Cincinnati, Columbus, Rochester, Buffalo and Pittsburgh. She'd left home after graduating high school and hadn't lived in Whedon or Erie since.

As if reading his mind, his mother said, "She'll find her place eventually." She slowed and added, "I'll tell Cessy to call about ski shopping."

"Thanks." And now they'd run out of things to talk about. "Well…" he said.

"Yes, I know. You're busy. But I'm glad you called. Your father and I miss you. We're always here, Seth. Doesn't matter what you need, we're here."

"Thanks." He clicked his phone shut.

Seth wished he knew how to make things better with his mother and father. But he didn't.

It had been ages since he'd talked to his parents about anything that mattered.

Most of the time, he was fine.

But sometimes, he missed them acutely.

Today was one of those times.

LAURA SLEPT HER MORNING AWAY, and thankfully, so did Jamie.

At two that afternoon she'd managed to get out of bed, feeling as if she'd been run over by a cement mixer, and took a shower.

It was amazing how restorative a shower could be.

She felt more herself as she sat in the rocker cradling the baby to her chest.

"Jameson Alexander Martin, III. My Jamie. It fits you, little man. I think your dad would have liked it, too. He was so sure we were going to have a girl, but he'd have been thrilled to have a son," she reassured him. She searched his tiny features, trying to find his father in them. But all she saw was Jamie.

"That's a good thing that you look like you and not someone else. You should look like you. You're your father's gift to me, but I don't ever want you to think you have to be anything other than yourself. That's all he'd have wanted. Be yourself, and be a good man."

The motion of the rocker soothed her as much as it did Jamie.

A knock on the door pulled her from her happy daydreaming. "That must be Seth. He called at lunch and insisted on driving us home. He's a bossy man, but you'll like him."

She called, "Come in, Seth. I was telling Jamie..." Her sentence faded as she found herself looking at Jay's parents instead of Seth.

She wanted to tell them to go immediately. The last time she'd seen them in a hospital...in this hospital...

She forced herself to be kind when she called them, to tell them about Jamie. And she would be kind now. "Mr. and Mrs. Martin."

"Thank you for letting us know the baby had arrived," Mrs. Martin said.

"You're welcome. It's what Jay would have wanted. We're leaving the hospital in a few minutes. I have a ride."

"I know," Mr. Martin said. "Seth's waiting in the hall. He wanted to give us a chance to see you."

"Oh." She wasn't sure if she should be pleased or annoyed that Seth was so considerate. Every fiber of her being wanted to call him in, but she knew she couldn't afford to start relying on him—on anyone.

"May I?" Mrs. Martin asked.

Laura nodded and handed Jay's mother the baby. "He looks like Jay did when he was a baby."

"I was trying to decide if he looked like his dad." She didn't add that she'd decided Jamie simply looked like himself.

"I have some baby pictures. I can make you copies. You should have some. Jamie should have some. He should know something about his father."

Laura tried not to take offense. She knew that Mrs. Martin didn't mean to imply she wouldn't tell Jamie about Jay. Still, she wanted to lash out. For Jay's sake, she simply said, "Thank you. That would be lovely."

Mrs. Martin extended the baby to her husband, but Jay's dad extended a finger at the baby, who held it. "He's got a grip. Just like Jay did."

"What did you name him?" Mrs. Martin asked.

"Jameson Alexander Martin, III, if that's okay with you. Since you're Jameson or Jim, Mr. Martin, and Jay was Jay, I thought I'd call him Jamie. I toyed with the idea of calling him Alexander, Xander for short, because I'll confess, I'm a huge Buffy fan, and always liked the name, but decided Jamie was better." She was babbling, and she knew it.

Mrs. Martin smiled. "Jamie. I like that."

"Then you don't mind that he has the last name Martin?" Laura had worried about that. She knew it might be easier if she and the baby had the same last name, but she and Jay had always intended for both Jamie and herself to be Martins. And even if she'd never be, she could give that legacy to her son. "I mean, Jay and I never..."

"Jay was married to you in his heart," Mrs. Martin said. "A piece of paper wouldn't have made his commitment or feelings any stronger. He'd love that you named the baby after him."

"Well, then, I can tell the nurse it's official. I was waiting until I checked with you."

"Laura, we need to talk—" Mrs. Martin said.

Laura couldn't do it. She couldn't talk to them right now. Her emotions were too close to the surface. "No. Not now, please. Not yet. I want to take my son home."

"You're right, I'm sorry. But later, please."

Laura didn't agree. She knew that Mrs. Martin wanted to talk about Jay's death. But she didn't. Couldn't. Images kept assaulting her, especially here in the hospital. The same hospital where Jay had been.

One week after Mrs. Martin had blown up at her about Jay, she'd called Laura, frantic. Laura remembered that day and the days that followed with frightening clarity.

In her experience, memories faded. They grew soft around the edges. But this memory stayed clear and strong. As if someone had adjusted the focus and held it tightly there. She'd gone back to that room, to that instant so many times.

"The doctor said he's dying. Despite the machines, his body's shutting down," Jay's mother sobbed over the phone.

Laura's first inclination was to tell her that Jay had been dead for more than a week, but she didn't. Instead, she said, "I'll be right there."

She'd visited every day, even though she knew in her heart that Jay was already dead.

She'd walked into the hospital, with its brightly lit lobby, and down the hall to the elevator bank, through the labyrinth of halls to Jay's room. And every day, it had been the same. His mother would be there and inform her there were no changes in his condition. No improvements.

When she said the words, Laura wanted to snap that of course there were no improvements, he was dead. How did you improve on that? She'd watch his chest rise and fall because of the ventilator, and know this wasn't what he wanted. And she'd blame his parents.

But she knew arguing with them wouldn't work, so she didn't say the words.

As she navigated the corridors, she admitted it could be for the last time. If his body was finally acknowledging what the doctors had known for a week, he'd let go and she wouldn't be back here. Instead, they'd take his body across the street to the funeral home.

She'd known it was coming, but thinking it made her shake.

She went into the room. The Martins were sitting on the opposite side of the bed. She gave them a brief nod, then took Jay's hand in hers, and gently kissed his cheek.

She waited the next hour until, finally, Jay went into cardiac arrest. A medical team came into the room and started trying to restart his heart. It was brutal and so senseless. "Stop," Laura cried. "Stop."

"No," Jay's mom choked out. "No. I can't lose him yet."

The team continued to work, then, without discussing it, they arrived at some sort of mutual agreement. One of the nurses listened to Jay's heart. "He's gone."

Mrs. Martin sank into cries of uncontrollable anguish. Mr. Martin stood stoically behind her without saying anything. Laura simply stood and looked at the lifeless body of the man she loved. He'd died.

And all their dreams for the future had died with him.

NOW, SIX MONTHS LATER, Jay's mother held his son. Cradling him. Cooing over him until the nurse came in with a wheelchair. "It's time to go now, Mom."

"We could take you home," Mrs. Martin offered.

"Thank you, but Seth is here for that."

"Laura, we'd really like to stop in and see you and the baby," Mrs. Martin asked apprehensively.

Laura didn't doubt they wanted to see the baby—Jay's son—but they'd proven six months ago that they didn't care about her. When they'd cut her out of the decisions about Jay, they'd treated her like the outsider she was. "That would be fine, though I'd appreciate it if you phoned first, in case Jamie's sleeping."

"If you need anything in the meantime, you call. Night or day, it doesn't matter," Mr. Martin said.

"I'm sure I won't, but thank you."

"Laura, I'm sorry. I—"

Laura knew the Martins hurt as much as she did. She knew they'd thought they were doing what was best for Jay, but in her heart, she couldn't get beyond the anger over what they'd put Jay through. She didn't want to hear her apologies. She didn't want to have this conversation, so she cut her off. "The nurse is waiting, Mrs. Martin."

Jay's mother looked disappointed, but nodded. "Yes, yes. I'll call in a few days."

"That would be fine."

"Laura," Mr. Martin said. "We really are sorry."

"I really have to go now, Mr. Martin. I don't want to make Seth wait any longer."

"Yes. Of course."

Slowly, Mrs. Martin handed the baby back to Laura and let Mr. Martin lead her from the room. Laura waited to feel guilt, anger or even pity for Jay's parents. She felt a mixture of all those emotions, but couldn't sort them out. At least not yet. She stared at her son instead and let the rush of love calm her. Center her.

Moments later, as Laura settled herself in the wheelchair, Seth was there. "You okay?"

She nodded. "Fine, fine. Why wouldn't I be?" She realized how defensive she sounded and added, "Really, I'm fine."

Seth's expression said he didn't believe her, but he let it go. "Come on then. Let's get this little guy home."

The nurse packed up a cart with Laura's bag and the flowers that the teachers at school had sent, and the ones that Jay's group had sent.

Laura had given Seth a key to the house to get the car seat for her, and he already had it installed like an old pro in the backseat of the truck. When she commented, he said, "The police department pairs up with the different organizations in town and does car seat checks for parents, so I've had a lot of practice."

With Seth's help, she got into the truck. As he closed the door, the cloying scent of flowers was overpowering. That's how Jay's funeral had smelled. Seth drove past Kloecker's Funeral Home. Sitting in a car that smelled of flowers, having seen Jay's parents and now driving past the funeral home was too much. Laura felt tears well up in her eyes. She turned toward the window, not wanting Seth to see her cry.

The smell of flowers. That's what stood out most in her memory of Jay's funeral.

Lines of people. Some she knew, some she didn't. All hugging her and expressing their sympathy.

That very nice funeral director who seemed to sense the tension between her and the Martins. Though they'd offered to let her sit in the limo with them after the service on the way to the cemetery, she declined. She'd opted to drive alone. Standing amidst all those strangers, listening to the minister talk about seasons, and how it was Jay's time, she'd wanted to scream: no. No, it wasn't his time. This shouldn't be his place.

He should be alive.

He should be here.

With her and his newborn son.

Tears ran freely down her cheeks as she stared out the window heading home with her fatherless son.

CHAPTER SIX

SETH KNEW LAURA WAS UPSET about the chief and his wife's visit, but he didn't know what to say. Laura and Jamie were both quiet on the ride home.

As they pulled into her driveway, Seth broke the silence. "I'll confess, I let JT into the house to finish Jamie's mural."

"She didn't have to do that."

"But she wanted to." He got Laura's bags and the flowers, while she got the baby.

They walked into the house and sniffed. "What's that?" she asked.

"Beef stew. It's in the Crock-Pot, so it's ready whenever you're hungry, and there will definitely be leftovers for tomorrow." He paused. "You do like stew, right?"

"I do. But, Seth, you didn't have to."

She was wrong. He did have to. Oh, he wanted to walk away. He'd stayed with her at the hospital, he'd been there for her while she gave birth. That should be enough. More than enough. But rather than leaving, he followed her farther into the house.

"It's just stew," he said. "I work tonight and wanted to be sure you were fed. I remember when my mother brought home my youngest sister. We were all adopted, so Mom hadn't given birth... She said those late-night feedings did her in. All us older kids pitched in and helped. I wanted to do the same for you."

He was certain Laura would protest that she could manage on her own, but all she said was, "Thank you. I think I'm going to put Jamie down in his bedroom."

"Wait till you see what JT did." He saw her delight as she studied JT's wall.

"Look how she managed the bubble tree. She's right, it's so much harder than an apple tree. It's beautiful." She seemed deep in thought, then asked, "When did you let JT in?"

"This morning. She called about nine and said since there was no school, she wanted to get the mural done."

"She lied."

"What?"

"There was school today," Laura explained. "I called in last night and my sub took over for me."

"She lied," he repeated. It hadn't occurred to him that JT would do it to his face. He felt stupid. He knew enough people in the school district now that he should have called and checked out her story.

He was still processing the information as Laura put the sleeping baby down in the crib and covered him. "Welcome home, Jamie."

Seth was mesmerized by the sight. There were no thoughts of his past, of his what-might-have-beens. His world had narrowed to Laura gazing at the baby. He couldn't tear himself away.

Laura grabbed the baby monitor and led him from the room.

"So what are we going to do about JT?" Seth asked, returning to full-on cop mode, which was a far more comfortable feeling than whatever it was he'd felt watching Laura with Jamie.

"Well, skipping school will definitely mean more detention," she said as she walked into the living room. "I'll talk to the principal next week. I know it's out of the ordinary, but I'm hoping that he'll let her do her detention here at home with me, at least for a few weeks, until I'm comfortable taking Jamie out. Then I can meet her at school after classes."

"So you're still going to work with her?"

She nodded, then sank back into the couch, curling up on herself. "I'm going to try."

She looked tired. Which was no wonder. She gave birth a day ago. Seth got up, pulled an afghan from the back of the couch and covered her up.

She smiled. "Thanks."

"You're sure you can manage JT and the baby?"

"I might not know much about this motherhood thing yet, but I suspect that as much as I love Jamie, I'm going to need more than his company to keep me busy." She yawned.

"Speaking of company. I know the guys from Jay's group plan to stop in. Thought I'd give you the heads-up."

"They won't give up, those guys."

"Jay was well liked. I didn't know him really, but everyone on his group speaks highly of him." She didn't say anything, but he could see the tears welling up in her eyes and wanted to change topics.

"Can I do anything else?" he asked.

"No, Jamie and I are fine. Sometimes I get so wrapped up in missing Jay that I forget that other people are missing him, too. I'll remember when they come over next time. And you've done more than I had a right to expect. I want to thank you for taking me to the hospital and staying. I don't know what I'd have done without you. I thought I could do it on my own, but..." She blinked her eyes hard, as if to fight back tears.

Seth thought most of the time he pulled off the tough-guy routine, but the sight of a woman's tears could destroy the facade in an instant—especially if it was Laura crying.

"Laura, I have no doubts that you could have managed on your own if you'd had to." He resisted the urge to brush away the one tear that had escaped to run down her cheek.

"Thank you. Sometimes I don't feel like I could."

"Well, if you forget, I'll remind you. Are you certain that I can't do anything else before I go?"

"I'd really love to take a shower in my own bathroom, but I don't want Jamie to wake up here alone. Could you wait a few minutes and listen for him? I know I'll eventually have to risk him crying while I shower, but not today."

"No, not today. I'll stay until you're settled." He had his uniform in the car, so he didn't need to go home before he started his shift.

Laura got up gingerly from the couch, walked over to his chair and kissed his cheek. "Great. I won't be long."

He heard doors opening and closing, and finally he could hear the sound of water coming from the bathroom. He ran a finger over the spot she'd kissed. Before he could dwell on why he wished the very platonic kiss was more than that, he heard the baby stirring on the monitor.

Seth hurried down the hall and leaned over the crib. Jamie stared at him. He picked the baby up and went to sit in the rocking chair.

He murmured a song near Jamie's ear, until the sound of clapping pulled him from the song. Laura was standing in the doorway, wearing a pair of sweats and a sweatshirt, with her damp hair twisted into a messy bun. "That was lovely."

He felt self-conscious. "I don't normally sing for audiences, well, other than babies."

"Hmm, maybe you should start?"

He didn't know what to say to that, so he simply skirted the compliment.

"Having so many siblings must be why you look like an old pro rocking Jamie, while I still worry about dropping him or goofing up."

"You're a natural. You'll feel like a pro in a couple days. But you can always call me if you need anything. Night or day. I'm on second shift the rest of the month and don't get off until ten or eleven. When you account for wind-down time, I'm up late."

He stood carefully and handed Jamie to her. She didn't look nervous or like a novice at all. She looked like a mom as she took her son and sank into the rocking chair.

"Speaking of work, I'd better go."

Jamie squawked and Seth laughed. "I think he's hungry, and while I can help with many things, I can't help with that." He leaned down and kissed her on the cheek without thinking. The fact that he'd done it surprised him, and despite the fact Laura had done as much earlier, she looked as startled as he was. He hurried toward the door. "I'll leave the spare key on the hall table."

"Maybe you should hang on to it? I don't have a spare key with anyone else, and if I have the new mom brain-dead moments and lock myself out, it would be nice to have someone who could come let me back in."

Seth nodded. "Sure. I'll hold on to it for now. Night, Laura."

"Night, Seth."

SETH PATROLLED THE STREETS of Erie.

It was after eleven, and Seth should have long since gone home, but third shift was running short on staff, so he agreed to work some overtime. Third shift could be a busy one, but the late November night was crisp and cold. So much so that even the worst of the nighttime elements preferred staying inside.

He drove by Laura's house and wondered, not for the first time, why they'd kissed. Granted, they weren't exactly steamy kisses. They were about as platonic as kisses could get. But despite the fact they barely qualified as kisses, he kept coming back to them. Worse, he kept wishing there were more.

Seth hadn't been with any woman since Allie. And if he were going to jump back into that particular pool, he couldn't pick a worse person to dive in with than Laura, who was a brand new mother, as well as in mourning.

Thinking about Laura was too confusing, so he turned his thoughts to JT. He'd have to leave a little early for work on Monday and go to the school to check on her. Ever since assuming his new responsibilities as school liaison, he'd come to believe that if everyone took an interest in just one kid who wasn't theirs, the world would be a better place.

His radio squawked. "Erie to Lima Eight."

"Lima Eight," he answered.

"Go to Kennedy School's playground and assist units on scene."

"Lima Eight, copy. En route." And that's what he got for even thinking it might be a quiet evening.

A few minutes later he pulled up to the school's playground. O'Donaldson and Hawley had two boys in the back of their cruiser. "We caught them spray-painting the school," O'Donaldson said. "We need to take them in. These other four," he nodded at two girls and a boy standing next to the car. "We found them sitting on the swings, talking. Unfortunately, it's way after curfew." Erie had instituted a 10:00 p.m. school night curfew a few years ago, and in Seth's opinion it was a great policy.

"They need to go home," Hawley said.

Seth nodded. "I'll get them all home while you deal with our graffiti artists."

"Thanks, Seth."

"No problem." He walked up to the four. "The officers explained you all broke curfew?"

The boy took a half step forward and replied, "Yes, sir."

Seth looked beyond the boy to the group of girls. "JT?"

"Hey, Lieutenant." Rather than looking embarrassed or at least apologetic, she gave him a cocky look that set his teeth on edge. She was back in her goth apparel. Black on black, with her piercings in and her makeup heavy. She hadn't dressed this severely in a while and he'd forgotten the look.

"You and I will discuss this after we've taken your friends home."

JT nodded, her expression cocky and unconcerned.

Seth turned his attention back to the other kids. "You knew about curfew?"

"Yes, sir. I needed to see Lisa. She's our foreign exchange student."

"She lives with me," the other girl piped in. "And she's going home tomorrow. Joel and Lisa have been dating and they wanted to say goodbye." The girl sighed, then added, "JT was here keeping me company."

Seth got their names and addresses and dropped the girls off first, leaving Joel in the back of the cruiser and JT in the front.

"My mom is going to kill me," Tammy said to no one in particular, as they headed toward her house. "Lisa, you're actually kind of lucky you're getting on a plane tomorrow. She can't ground you if you're back in France."

Seth hid his smile as he knocked on the door.

A dark-haired woman answered a moment later. "Hello, Officer?"

He saw her shock when she spotted the girls. "Tammy and Lisa, you told me you would finish packing and then go to bed."

"Ma'am, I'm Lieutenant Keller. And we found Tammy and Lisa out at the school playground."

"You what?" The woman looked from Seth to the girls then back to Seth. "Come in, please, Officer."

They all stepped into the foyer.

"Maman Annette, I only wanted to say goodbye to Joel one more time. You can't know how hard it is to be *arraché* from the one you love," she said with a great deal of drama. "Old people like you have forgotten what it's like to really be in love. Joel, *c'est ma vie!* He is my destiny."

Tammy's mom tried valiantly to hide a smile, and Tammy simply shook her head. "Lisa tells me all the time that Americans don't know anything about love."

Seth cleared his throat. "Be that as it may, breaking curfew is serious. And, ma'am, you should know that two of the boys the girls were with were taken down to the station for vandalism."

"Not Joel, Maman Annette!" Lisa assured her.

Seth nodded his agreement. "No, not Joel. He'll be escorted home next."

"Are the girls in trouble?" Tammy's mother asked.

"I could write a warning up, but since Lisa is leaving tomorrow, and I'm assuming that Tammy here has learned her lesson?"

Tammy nodded her head with more vigor than the answer required.

"Well, then I'm inclined to give you all a verbal warning this time. Next time, though..." He'd found that a threat was more effective if left to a teen's imagination.

"There won't be a next time, sir," Tammy assured him.

"Officer, may I say goodbye one more time?" Lisa asked. "After all my poor Joel was arrested in the name of love. It's *très romantique.*"

He knew he should be stern and say no, but he couldn't quite manage it. "Go ahead," he told the girl.

Lisa bolted down the stairs and Tammy hung behind. "I only went to the park to keep her out of trouble. I called JT to meet me because it's awkward being around that." She nodded at Lisa and Joel.

All three of them watched as the girl hugged the boy.

"You know, Lisa loves reading romances. By the time she gets home, she'll be telling the story of the boy who did jail time for her. I'm going to my room, Mom. And, Officer?" Seth looked at the girl. "Thank you."

She disappeared up the stairs.

"She seems like a good kid," Seth said.

"She is," Tammy's mom agreed. "So's Lisa. Tammy hasn't really fallen in love yet, but Lisa..." She smiled. "Well, her romance with Joel reminded me of what it was like to be that young and that much in love. A time when you thought you breathed in and out because of someone else. Do you remember what that was like, Lieutenant?"

Seth had met Allie his freshman year, and for him, it was like that. "Yes, I remember."

Lisa returned, her eyes wet with tears. "*Merci,* sir."

"You're welcome, Lisa." He nodded to Tammy's mom. "Good night, ma'am."

"Thank you, Officer."

He glanced back as he walked to his cruiser and saw Tammy's mother envelop Lisa in a hug. It made him think of his own mom.

She'd been on his mind a lot lately.

JT silently glared at him as he got back into the cruiser and drove to Joel's house. Seth threw the cruiser into Park and shut off the engine. JT still slouched in the front seat, not looking at him. He let the boy out of the vehicle and they walked toward his front door.

"Sir," Joel said. "Before we go in, I want to say thanks again for letting Lisa and me say goodbye."

Seth stared at the boy. He was rail-thin and gangly, and had the slightest dusting of hair on his lip, but an adult expression of resignation.

"Believe it or not, I remember what it was like to be young, stupid and in love."

Joel expressed surprise. "You're not going to tell me I'm too young?"

"No, kid, I'm not going to tell you that at all. I don't think there's an age requirement for loving someone. Usually, it happens when you least expect it."

"I'm still not sure what Lisa saw in me. I'm not one of the cool kids. I'm in marching band and take AP classes. I'd never thought I'd be the kind of guy that the cute, French foreign exchange student falls for."

"But you are the kind of guy that a smart, insightful girl falls for."

"And now, I'm losing her. I knew we'd have to say goodbye, but I wasn't ready for it. She was supposed to stay until the end of term, but her grandmother's sick and she needs to go home early."

"I don't know if we're ever ready to say goodbye to someone we love, kid." The words he'd intended for the boy rebounded, and far too close to home. Seth needed this conversation to end. "Let's go talk to your parents."

"My mom's not going to be as cool as Tammy's mom," Joel told him as he crawled from the backseat.

"No?"

"I'm all she has, and she worries a lot." Joe's voice dropped, as if he were imparting some great secret. "She's going to be a mess."

"So why did you sneak out if you knew it might make her worry?" Seth asked as they walked up to the pleasant-looking brick bungalow.

"Have you ever loved a girl, sir?" the boy asked again.

Allie had been it for him. But a memory of Laura popped into his mind and guilt struck him.

"I don't have a key," Joel said. "I was going to go back in through my bedroom window."

"We'll knock."

Seth heard someone at the door, then it flew open. "Joel?"

"Hi, Mom."

"Hi, Mom?" The woman's voice rose about an octave. "Hi, Mom? You went to bed early because you had a headache."

"Yeah, but I didn't. I climbed out the window to go see Lisa one more time."

"And unfortunately, ma'am..." Seth let the ma'am hang there, and the woman replied, "Jan. Jan Vesser."

"Ms. Vesser, the problem is not only did Joel break the city's curfew, two of his friends are at the station now being booked for graffiti."

"Joel?"

"I didn't do it, Mom. I never would. You know that."

Joel's mom raked her fingers through her hair. "I might have known it once upon a time, but I don't know you anymore."

"They were at the playground with me, so I could say goodbye to Lisa, then they pulled out paint and started messing around. We didn't do anything. Me, Lisa and Tammy sat on the swings."

"I told you they're bad news. I told you—"

Seth asked, "Ma'am, can I speak with you alone?"

"Go up to your room, Joel. I'll come talk to you in a minute."

Joel made a dash for what he assumed was the kitchen.

"Ma'am, he's in love," Seth said. "He did something stupid, but wasn't causing any real trouble."

"We were so close, then he started hanging with these boys, and this girl and..." She looked distraught. "I don't know him anymore."

"He's a teenager. I think that's par for the course. He needs to know that there are rules and boundaries, but that ultimately, you're on his side."

"I want what's best for him. When he was little, I dreamed he'd be a doctor and make the world better. Now, I want him to pass ninth grade and not be brought home by the cops again." This woman—so worried about her son, tears in her eyes—could have been his mother worrying about him. "I would do anything to give my son an easier life than I had. I wanted you to know that." She turned away from him.

"Ms. Vesser? Ma'am, sometimes your dreams for your child aren't the same as their dreams. Sometimes, they have to follow their own path, even if it's not the direction you'd have chosen for them."

She faced Seth. "I should let him be with this girl?"

"The girl in question is leaving. What I'm saying is you need to talk, and even more importantly, you need to listen and show him you understand. He thinks this girl is it for him...the one." Memories pounded at Seth of a time when he felt that way. "Maybe she is."

"I just want what's best for him."

"Do you mind if I check back with you in a week or so?" Seth found himself asking.

"Really?"

He reached into his shirt pocket. "Really. And here's my card. You call if you need me before then."

"Thanks, Officer."

"It's my job, ma'am."

"I think you're wrong. Bringing him home might have been your job, but the rest of it?" She shook her head. "I don't think that falls under a cop's duties. Thanks."

Seth got into the cruiser, turned to JT and simply said, "Speak."

"I screwed up again. Big shock."

He waited without saying anything.

"Mom has a new guy at the house, so when Tammy called, I went. I thought I'd give them some privacy."

"Does she know you left the house?"

JT didn't respond and he silently waited. He thought he was going to have to break the stalemate, when she finally said, "Ms. Watson called to say thanks for the mural. I'm glad she's had her kid. Now I can go back to regular detentions where they just ignore you as long as you're quiet."

Seth felt a flash of insight into JT reverting to her old habits. "JT, Ms. Watson hasn't fogotten about you. I'm sure—"

"Just take me home, Lieutenant, okay? Or write me up, or take me back to the station."

"JT—"

"If you're not going to throw me in jail again, then take me home and read my mom the riot act like you did the other kids' parents. Just don't lecture me to death. You've already tortured me enough tonight."

"Tortured you?"

"You let Lisa and Joel say goodnight. Their gushing over each other had me on the verge of vomiting."

Seth put a hand over his mouth to cover his inadvertent chuckle. "Well, maybe some torture will remind you to toe the line. There are rules, and they're there for a reason. My job is to see to it you follow them. Not to be a hard-ass, but to keep you safe. Speaking of rules, did you ever hear the ones about not lying to cops, and not skipping school?"

"Huh?" JT said, playing innocent.

"The other day when you finished the mural?"

"I just wanted to get it done, okay? Ms. Watson's class was the only one where I didn't feel like a loser. Now she's gone, and the sub they hired..." She let the sentence hang.

"The sub isn't like Ms. Watson," Seth filled in.

JT nodded.

"You know I have to turn you in for skipping school, right?"

"Yeah, whatever."

"It will probably mean a whole new set of detentions." JT didn't respond and Seth left her in silence while he drove her home.

As he walked her to the front door of her house, she said, "Don't tell Ms. Watson about tonight, okay? She's got enough to worry about with the new baby. She can just forget about me and get on with her life."

Seth shook his head. "I think you underestimate Ms. Watson. She won't forget about you."

JT snorted and stood by silently as he told her mother she'd broken curfew.

"Get to your room," her mother ordered.

JT shot him a look and then hurried up the stairs.

"Thanks for bringing her home, Officer. You don't know how hard it is to ride herd on a kid like JT. She's always being difficult."

"She simply needs someone to take an interest, ma'am." It was as tactful as Seth could manage. What he wanted to tell the woman was to stop mooning over men and pay attention to her daughter.

The woman didn't respond, other than to say good-night, as she shut the door.

The rest of the night was as quiet as he'd originally hoped. It was eight in the morning when he walked into his apartment. As if on cue, the phone rang. "Hello?"

"Oh, Seth, you're there. I thought I'd get your answering machine," his mother said. "I was going to leave you a message. Cessy's basketball team has a game next week in Erie. It's their Thanksgiving tournament. I know you said that you can't be with us on Thanksgiving because of work."

He felt a sense of guilt. He could have been there.

His mother continued, "I thought you might want to come. I know Cessy would be happy."

Maybe his guilt was what prompted him to say, "Yes, sure. I'll be there."

"Really?" his mom said, then hurried and gave him the information. "How are you?" she asked.

"Fine. And you?"

"Fine."

And that was that. He loved his parents beyond measure, but he had no answer to repair the rift with them. When Allie found out she was pregnant, she forced him to talk to his parents. And he had. They hadn't exactly discussed the past, but he'd been willing to begin again.

Then Allie and the babies had died and that beginning ended.

Every word of sympathy, every tear they'd shed at the funeral home seemed false.

They hadn't wanted him to marry Allie. They'd never approved. So, how could they mourn her loss?

He'd been so angry.

But today? He knew one thing for sure. He was homesick.

CHAPTER SEVEN

MONDAY AFTERNOON WAS BRIGHT, sunny and warm for Erie in November. Laura bundled six-day-old Jamie up and went to school.

She'd called the doctor's office to be sure it was okay to take him out, and the nurse on duty had promised that anything she felt up to doing was fine.

Well, Laura felt like getting out of the house. She was loving being home with Jamie, but she longed for some adult interaction, which is exactly what she got when her first stop was the teachers' lounge. Friends oohed and ahhed over the baby, and filled her in on school news.

Afterward, she met the principal, who consented to her continuing to work with JT at home. Her detention had been extended because she skipped school last week.

The end-of-the-day bell rang.

General detention was in the auditorium and she waved to Jodie, who was in charge. "Can I steal JT for a few minutes?"

"Sure. Need me to watch Jamie?"

Laura felt better for being out, but she wasn't ready to separate from her son, even for a few minutes.

"Thanks, but he's fine." She spotted JT sitting in the back row. "JT?" she called.

JT hurried after her into the hall. She spoke rapidly. "Ms. Watson, I didn't think you'd be in."

JT looked at the baby. "He's awfully tiny, Ms. Watson. How come you brought him out to see me?"

"I was worried about you. And I had an idea. Mr. Asti agreed, and we talked to your mom who gave her permission. All that's left is to see if you agree."

"That's a lot of agreeing." JT eyed her suspiciously. "What's it about? My skipping school?"

"In a way. I suggested that you walk to my house after school each day. I clocked it on the way here, and it's almost a half a mile on the nose. I walked it until the weather got too bad and I was too round. Anyway, you walk over and serve your detention with me at my house. Your mom can pick you up on her way home. I'd offer to come into school, but Jamie's so little. I worried about bringing him out today. Anyway—"

"Hang on, you still want me to do detentions with you?" Despite the heavy makeup and piercings, JT appeared little-girl surprised.

Laura nodded.

"I thought once you had the baby, you'd forget all about me."

"That's not likely to happen...ever. You're stuck with me caring, like it or not. I see so much potential in you. I don't want to see you throw it all away without a thought. If you could read better—"

For a moment, Laura thought she was really reaching the girl, but when she mentioned reading, JT's expression hardened. "For what? To prove to you I'm not stupid? Listen, Ms. Watson, I don't have to prove anything to you or anyone else."

"No, but maybe you need to prove something to yourself. Listen, I'm just an art teacher, but—"

"Ms. Watson, I never thought of you as *just* an art teacher."

"And I've never thought of you as *less* than remarkable. I don't think you read well, and the fact you've made it to high school shows how smart you are. Let me help you, JT."

Laura wanted to explain to JT, to make her see in herself what she saw so clearly. "Maybe, it's because I am an art teacher."

"Huh?"

"I'm trained to look beyond the surface. Paintings, drawings, sculpture, aren't simply subjects, there's always some emotion, some story behind them. I look for that, and try to see what's beneath it. I see the image you try to project." She reached out and gently touched JT's eyebrow ring. "But beneath that hard image, I see a smart, talented girl who's capable of so much. Let me help you."

JT didn't look happy. "I think you're nuts, but fine. I'll come serve my detention at your house."

"Thanks."

"Yeah, well, don't thank me yet. I mean every other teacher here in school has written me off. The fact that you haven't makes you crazier than all of them."

"Hey, I had a baby. I deserve some crazy time. So, head back into detention here today, but my house tomorrow, right after school lets out, okay?"

"You're not going to give up, are you?"

"Not a chance."

"Tomorrow then."

Despite JT's unenthused expression, Laura thought she saw a flicker of something else in the girl's eyes.

Something that looked like hope.

TUESDAY AND WEDNESDAY went by fast. It was as if time had blurred. Jamie wanted to eat every three hours like clockwork. Laura listened to her lactation consultant and tried to sleep whenever he did. Except when JT came over.

Those first two days they read together.

JT wasn't illiterate, but her reading skills hadn't progressed beyond a grade-school level.

"...it's like a code," Laura explained on Thursday. "You learn what letters say when they're together."

"They didn't teach sounding it out. They taught us whole words. I can see those, but I don't know how to figure out new ones."

"That's what phonics does. It breaks words into syllables."

JT studied the page in front of her. "*G*—" she pronounced a hard G "—net-ics."

"That *G* sounds like a *J*."

"See, it doesn't work."

"Hard or soft. It's always one or the other, so, if it's not hard, then it's soft. Say the word with a soft gee."

She said it with a soft *G*. "Ge-net-ics." She paused. "Genetics."

"That's right."

"Okay, let's finish this science."

It took an hour, but JT managed the next three pages, and then they completed the worksheet. "I did it."

"You did."

"It took a long time."

"Yes, but it's not really how long it takes, it's getting it done that counts. Michelangelo took four years to paint the Sistine Chapel. It's a masterpiece."

"My science isn't a masterpiece."

"But you read the chapter and you did the work. Just think, you can go to school after the Thanksgiving break and hand in the homework."

JT smiled. "I know tomorrow's out 'cause it's Thanksgiving, but can we meet on Friday?"

"You know you don't have to serve a detention on a vacation day, but I'd love if you came over. Maybe in the morning?"

"Yeah. That's good. I'll see you then. You go get Jamie, and I'll let myself out."

"Night, JT. Make sure you do your math."

"Math is easy, Ms. Watson. One plus one always equals two. It's not like English where letters change their sounds on a whim. Hard *G*'s, soft *G*'s. It's a mess." JT laughed. "Happy Thanksgiving."

Happy Thanksgiving. Laura knew it was coming, but had managed not to think about it. Now, she'd have the whole day tomorrow to not think about it.

She hurried down the hall to Jamie, who was still—well, not full-out crying. It was more of a hey-I'm-awake, where-are-you?

"Hey, Laura! JT let me in," Seth called from the front door.

"Just a minute," she called.

Seth. She hadn't seen him at all this week. They'd exchanged voice mail, but she figured he was easing away from her, and she didn't blame him. One minute, they'd been declaring they were allies over JT, the next he was in the birthing room with her. And then they'd offered each other those friendly kisses. Kisses she was not going to reflect on...or repeat.

She'd go out, tell him she was fine, and then send him on his way.

She cradled Jamie as she went into the living rom and found Seth, in uniform, waiting for her. "On your way to work, or from?"

SETH DRANK IN THE SIGHT of Laura. She looked good.

They'd played phone-tag, but he'd purposely stayed away. He hadn't planned on seeing her today. It was better for both of them if they had some distance. She'd said that repeatedly, and he believed it. Hell, he needed to get back to the orderly life he'd built for himself. But here it was, Wednesday, and he'd found himself pulling into her driveway on the way to work.

Staying away hadn't kept her off his mind. If anything, she'd been on it more than ever. He thought that maybe if he saw her and reassured himself that she was fine, he'd be able to maintain that distance. Able to stop thinking about two insignificant pecks on the cheek.

"Seth, to work, or on the way home?" she repeated as she patted the baby's back with the quiet confidence of an old pro.

"To work. I wanted to stop and check on you both." He held out his hands to Jamie. "May I?"

Standing next to Laura, holding the baby, Seth felt as if a rubber band that had been pulled too tight finally released. "Hey, big guy, how's your week going?"

"So, what brings you here?"

He looked up from Jamie and tried to remember his excuse for stopping in. He spotted a cornucopia on her table. "I wanted to see what you were doing tomorrow for Thanksgiving."

"Nothing." She hurriedly added, "You know with a brand-new baby, I don't want to go out anywhere."

"I had the day off, but traded it with a friend who has small kids at home."

Laura frowned. "That's nice, but what about your family?"

"I'm going to see them Friday. My sister has a tournament in town. Want to come along?"

Again, that's not what he'd intended to say. But he realized that having Laura along would give him a buffer. He missed his family, dammit, but when he saw them it only reminded him that things had changed and he didn't know how to change them back.

"You want me to come to your sister's tournament?"

"If not to the actual game, maybe after? We'll be going out to eat. I thought you might like to get out of the house," he ended lamely.

"What about Jamie?"

"Maybe the chief and his wife could babysit? I know they'd love to."

"Oh, you know?" Jamie gave a little whine, which gave Laura reason to take him back. Her tone was terse as she asked, "You've been talking to him about me? About Jamie?"

"Nothing more than saying you're both fine."

"And you're still trying to forge some kind of relationship between me and Jay's parents, and that's not going to happen."

"They're the baby's grandparents," Seth said softly.

"Right, but they're nothing to me. I won't keep them from seeing him, but I'm not ready to have them babysit."

"So bring him along."

She took a deep breath and stared at the baby. "I don't know."

"My family would love it." Seth realized that it wasn't just his family—he'd love it. He'd missed Laura and he hated the thought of her being alone on Thanksgiving.

"Can I think about it?"

"Sure. I'll check in with you tomorrow. Before I go, do you need anything?"

"No, I'm fine. I've got everything under control." She said the words as if she were trying to convince herself as much as him. "JT just left. Of course, you know that since she let you in. She..." Laura jumped into a discussion about the reason they'd formed their alliance.

Discussing JT was easy, familiar ground. Twenty minutes later, Seth said, "I've got to go, or I'll be late." He headed toward the front door.

Laura followed him, cradling Jamie. "Have a good night, Seth."

Without thinking, he leaned down and kissed her forehead. "Thanks."

She looked startled.

Hell, he'd kissed her again. Apologizing for the chaste kiss would only give it significance, so he simply said, "I'll check with you again about Friday," and out into the cold he went, trying not to think about having kissed Laura again. He'd done it without thought and it felt natural.

This fact disturbed him more than the kiss itself.

He went on three domestic calls. The holidays certainly brought out the best in people. He should have been too busy to think about Laura, but thoughts of her kept intruding—the image of her holding Jamie, the look of surprise on her face when he'd planted that platonic kiss on her forehead, even the thought of her on her own with Jamie for Thanksgiving.

He couldn't seem to stop thinking about her and worrying about her. Which is why he was on her doorstep at noon the next day.

SETH PACKED UP HIS CAR and was on Laura's doorstep at noon. She looked tired and...well, rumpled.

"Happy Thanksgiving!" he practically shouted.

"Quiet," she whispered. "Jamie's asleep. I don't know if it was colic, or simply a bad night, but the good news is, I am reacquainted with what's available on late-night television, and I am thinking about ordering a new kitchen Wonder Gadget."

Seth nodded at the box in his hands. "Speaking of kitchens, mind if I make myself at home in yours?" He didn't wait for her response, but simply went there. This was crazy. He hadn't intended to come here today, yet here he was...again. He was using the holiday as an excuse, when deep down he knew he'd have shown up here regardless. Staying away had been hard. Too hard.

"What's in the box, Keller?"

"Well, I have to be at work in a few hours, but I decided that I couldn't really let the holiday go by without a traditional dinner."

In the kitchen, he began emptying his box. There was a box of stuffing, a can of cranberry sauce, a frozen pumpkin pie, a box of frozen mashed potatoes, a container of whipped topping and a small, rectangular foil pan.

Laura pointed at the foil. "What's that?"

He cracked the foil top. "That is a turkey loaf."

"Huh?"

"It said it was a hundred percent turkey, but it didn't say what part of the turkey. It does, however, make its own gravy. But just in case..." He reached into the box and presented a jar of turkey gravy to her. "Ta da." He sounded like his brother, Zac, but channeling Zac was easier than being himself. Zac was easygoing and charming—everything Seth wasn't.

Seth smiled as Laura laughed. "And here I was going to have a microwave turkey dinner."

"Oh, this is quite the step up. I started the turkey loaf at home, but it still needs time in the oven. I can have dinner ready in an hour." He turned on the oven and put the turkey pan into it, then asked, "Pots?"

She pointed. "Seth, JT keeps asking me why I care, and I keep telling her it's because I do. Her question frustrates me because I don't know how to explain why I feel compelled to help her. But I find myself wanting to ask you the same thing. Why are you here? I mean, I get that you feel the same compulsion to help JT. We both think she's special. But this isn't about JT. And staying with me while I had Jamie wasn't about her, either. We agreed to be allies, but this—" she waved her hand at the makeshift Thanksgiving meal "—and Jamie's birth, well, they're more than that. I'm no charity case, and I don't want you here because you feel your boss—"

He took her by the shoulders and said, "Stop right there, Laura." Zac would know what to say, but Seth didn't have a clue. He tried to find the right words. "You're no charity case, and I'm not here because of any sense of obligation. Yes, I checked in on you at first because of JT. But now, this isn't about that. I think you can use a friend. I know I can. So, let's say I'm here because I get what it's like to be lost without someone. Because..."

He dropped her shoulders and pulled a can of cranberry sauce off the counter and placed it on her can opener. With his back toward her, he said, "I was a baby that no one wanted. I know that Jamie has you, and he's so lucky for that. But since Jay can't be here for him, I'd like to be. I want him to have as many people as possible in his life watching out for him."

"That would be—"

The doorbell rang, and Laura groaned as she headed toward the front door, muttering about noise and sleeping babies, while all Seth felt was a sense of relief. Channeling his brother's openness was exhausting.

Seth continued preparing his not-quite gourmet dinner. He could hear murmurs, then footsteps coming down the hall.

"Seth, look who's here." Laura's voice was flat, devoid of emotion, as she stood in the doorway to the kitchen.

"Sir. Mrs. Martin. Happy Thanksgiving," Seth said.

"To you, too. Laura said you stopped in to cook for her."

Mrs. Martin frowned at the box of frozen mashed potatoes.

"I knew she didn't want to go out today and thought it was a way to be sure she got dinner. It says they're real—the mashed potatoes," he offered. "But Laura and I aren't sure about the turkey. We've decided to not ask too many questions."

"We stopped in to see if she'd reconsider dinner with us," the chief said, "but we can see that she's well taken care of."

"I'm sorry Jamie's sleeping," Laura said.

"Do you mind if we tiptoe in and see him before we go?" Mrs. Martin asked. "We won't wake him."

"Sure."

As soon as the Martins had disappeared down the hall, Seth said, "I didn't know they were coming."

Laura nodded. "I didn't think you did."

"You okay?"

"I was remembering last Thanksgiving when Jay and I had dinner with them. Mrs. Martin asked me to call her Mom and I said no, not until after the wedding. She helped me plan the wedding. I don't have my mom and she only had Jay, so she volunteered. She said that she didn't think she'd ever have a chance to plan a wedding. She cried and hugged me, and at that moment I wanted to call her Mom more than anything in the world. It was such a happy day. And now?" She brushed away tears. "Sorry. New-mom hormones."

"You're going to have to work things out with them sometime, for Jamie's sake," he added quickly. "But it doesn't have to be today. Let me help."

"Seth, you don't have—"

"We started out as allies, but now we're friends, remember? This isn't about the chief, the baby or JT. I'm your friend. And like I said, I know how hard it can be to deal with people when you're feeling shredded from a loss."

Laura nodded. "Thanks. I think I'll lie down for a few minutes."

She walked past him and stopped short, stood on tiptoe and kissed his cheek. "Friends."

Damn. Another kiss. That was four. Four totally innocent kisses. The Europeans kissed each other casually all the time, he assured himself. It didn't mean anything.

But if it didn't mean anything, why did he feel as if he'd just cheated on Allie?

He was saved from delving any deeper when the Martins appeared. "Where's Laura?"

"The baby was up all night. She's napping while I finish making dinner."

The chief nodded.

Mrs. Martin said, "Please thank her for letting us spend time with the baby, even if he was sleeping. I'll call soon."

"I'll tell her, ma'am."

"How about your family?" the chief asked.

"I'm working second, so I told them to eat without me. The whole bunch are coming into town tomorrow for that big basketball tourney. I'll see them then."

"Good. Family matters, Seth. Our job can make it difficult, but that only means we have to try all the harder. Because when life is over, I don't think anyone says, 'I wish I'd worked more overtime,' rather than 'I wish I'd had more time with my family.'"

Mrs. Martin rushed from the room.

The chief looked stricken. "And that's what you call, putting your foot in it. I assure you, though, I regret not having more time with Jay, and would do anything if I could have even one more minute with my son. Or if I could go back and undo this rift with Laura, I would. She was like a daughter to us."

"Give her time, sir."

"I don't have any other option, do I?" Resigned, he started down the hall after his wife, then turned around and said, "Happy Thanksgiving, Seth. Please tell Laura I said the same to her. And tell her Adele and I have our lists for dinner, and at the top of each one are her and Jamie's name."

Seth wasn't sure what lists the chief was talking about, but said, "I'll tell her, sir. Happy Thanksgiving."

Half an hour later, he heard Jamie stir, which was good because their impromptu meal was almost done.

He got Jamie and changed his diaper before gently knocking on Laura's door, which was ajar. She didn't call out and he nudged the door with his foot and saw her curled at the edge of the bed.

He stood and simply watched her for a minute.

When she was awake, she was formidable, whether she was fighting for JT, or caring for her son. Or even being angry with the chief. She was of average height, but now, she seemed dwarfed by the bed.

Cradling the baby in one hand, he gently tapped Laura's arm. "Laura, you need to wake up. Jamie's hungry."

She sat upright, blinking her eyes. "Seth?"

"Jamie woke up. He's changed, but hungry."

"Oh."

"Why don't you feed him. Our dinner should be ready when you're done."

Seth set the kitchen table. He found candles in the cupboard and lit them. The meal, while not exactly home-cooked, was close. They laughed as they chatted and ate.

Seth insisted on doing the dishes afterward.

Laura sat at the island, holding Jamie, watching him. "Seth, we forgot something."

"What?"

"We didn't say what we were thankful for. My family used to have actual lists. We'd write down what we were thankful for and save the list. Mom always said that those lists were her lifeline when she was feeling blue."

"That's what the chief meant."

"Pardon?" Laura asked.

Seth dried the bowl he'd nuked the potatoes in. "The chief told me to tell you that you and Jamie were at the top of their list."

"Oh." She didn't say anything else.

"Do you have a list this year?"

"No, I didn't make a list because I wasn't feeling very thankful, but today wasn't as hard as I thought it would be...thanks to you." She jumped up and grabbed a Post-it from the kitchen drawer and scribbled a few words on it. "There. Now I can put it in the box with the rest of my lists. And to make it official, I'll read it. I want to say I'm thankful for Jamie, for my time with Jay and for you. You've made everything easier."

She passed him the Post-it pad and pen and eyed him expectantly.

It had been a long time since Seth had concentrated on what he was thankful for. "I'm game. I'm thankful for finding my way back to old memories that give more pleasure than pain, and for making new memories that I'll treasure. I'm thankful for good friends and family."

He felt rather hypocritical saying he was thankful for his family. He could have gone to dinner with them, but working was easier. It suddenly felt like an excuse.

"About tomorrow?" he asked.

"You're sure your family wants someone else tagging along?"

He was sure he wanted someone else there. It was selfish of him, but he knew the Keller clan would be so enthralled with the baby and Laura, they'd forget all about him and he could fade comfortably into the background, which is where he preferred to be.

"I'm sure."

"Then yes, a night out would be nice. I'll drive myself and meet you there. That way if it's too much with Jamie I can go and not interrupt your time with your family."

Seth wanted to tell her he'd welcome the interruption, but in light of the Post-it he still held, he didn't.

He was thankful for his family. More specifically for his parents.

He was going to go tomorrow and try to show them all that.

CHAPTER EIGHT

LAURA RECONSIDERED agreeing to dinner with Seth's family. All day she'd thought about calling him and telling him that Jamie was too fussy. But the thing was, she sensed he wanted her there. And after everything he'd done for her, she couldn't walk away from that, so she went.

The Keller family was meeting at Joe Root's, one of her favorite Erie restaurants. It used to be at the base of the peninsula, but a few years ago, it had moved about half a mile up Peninsula Drive. Though it was in a new building, the owner had recreated the same hometown place she loved. She'd come here often with Jay.

Laura waited for the pain to follow the happy thought, but it never happened. The hostess pointed her to a sectioned-off area.

"Which table?" Laura asked.

"All of them."

Laura felt overwhelmed by the sheer quantity of people.

Seth spotted her right off. "Everyone, this is Laura Watson. Laura, this is..."

He gestured to a man wearing braces on his legs. "My brother, Dom."

"My sisters Layla," a smiling woman with curly auburn hair and skin a warm, bronze tone. "And May," who was older-looking than Layla, possibly Laura's own age of twenty-seven. She had long, straight coal-black hair and rather than smiling at Laura, she studied her.

Seth nodded at a younger girl with very curly dark hair, wearing jeans and a sweatshirt with a basketball team logo. "This is Cessy, who had the basketball game in town tonight."

"That's *Cecily*," his youngest sister said. "None of them can remember I'm not six anymore." She sounded totally exasperated, but winked at Laura to let her know she wasn't.

Laura laughed. "I'll try to remember that, *Cecily*," she promised.

Seth indicated a couple in the corner, the brown-haired man held a little boy on his lap. "That's my brother, Zac, and his wife Eli." Eli waved at Laura.

"Eli and I have met," Laura told Seth. She'd meant to tell him before, but kept getting sidetracked.

He nodded and said, "Nice. So you know one person other than me. That's their son, Johnny. And that's Colm. He works for my brother."

"I hadda come, 'cause me and Cessy is friends, and she needed me to cheer for her at her game. She's a rock star." Laura recognized immediately that Colm had special needs.

Seth laughed. "I used that term to describe my sister once, and Colm latched on to it."

"Yeah, 'cause Cessy's a rock star."

"That's Ariel and her daughter, Nora."

Ariel called out, "I'm not officially a Keller, but they've sort of adopted me and Nora, as well. Cessy's my best friend. And she likes it when I come to games to protect her from her brothers' abuse."

"Hey, we don't abuse her, do we, guys?" Zac and Dom echoed Seth's contention. "If anything, she's the bane of our existence."

"Don't push me, Seth," Cessy warned. "When you're the youngest, you learn to rely on family stories and gossip, otherwise you'd never have all the dirt you need to survive so many siblings."

"Yup, we feel for you, Cessy." Seth laughed. Then abruptly stopped. His genuine happiness was suddenly dimmed. "And finally, that's my mom and dad, Abe and Deborah Keller."

Mr. Keller looked as if he'd ridden straight out of a Western. Not a cowboy, but rather a mountain man. He was big, and his gray hair and beard were grizzly-looking. Mrs. Keller, on the other hand, was tiny and impeccably dressed. "Nice to meet you, Laura," she said, then she turned her gaze from Laura to Seth, and Laura saw pain in her eyes.

"I'll try to keep everyone straight," Laura vowed, though she knew it wouldn't be easy, and probably not even possible.

Seth showed her and Jamie to two empty seats on the opposite end of the table from his parents.

"Do you mind if I take Jamie out of his seat?" he asked.

"No, that's fine." That was the last she saw of her son for the next hour. He passed from Keller to Keller, being utterly adored as they all talked to and over each other in turn.

Laura took it all in and wondered what it would be like to have grown up in a family like the Kellers. Loud. Laughing. And loving. Their love for each other was palpable.

She ate her fish and chips and enjoyed listening to the snippets of conversation.

"...and I got into Mercyhurst University, too. Now, I have to decide where to go."

"...and yes, I'm a barista in Cleveland now. I liked Pittsburgh fine, but it was time to try a new city. I'm heading to Ireland this summer. I've got my backpack ready to go."

"...it's hard to see the guys come through the VA. They've done so much for our country, and I feel like my job is to put the pieces back together for them."

"Hey, lady." She looked up and Colm was standing there.

"I like to think I'm a lady, but you can call me Laura." She smiled at him.

"Yeah, and I'm Colm. I wanna hold the baby and Eli said she'd help me, but I told her I gotta ask first. Some moms get all worried that 'cause I'm special I can't hold babies, but I'm real careful, and I ain't never dropped one once. I held Nora and Johnny when they was little, and I

155

hold 'em now sometimes, but they're a lot more squiggly and that makes it harder, but I still ain't never dropped 'em. Zac and Eli will watch me, I promise."

She looked up at Zac, who nodded as if he could hear their conversation from the far end of the room.

"Colm, you may definitely hold Jamie. He's not very squiggly at all yet."

"Hey, thanks, lady. I'm gonna go take my turn before I miss it. If Mrs. Keller gets that baby, I ain't never gonna get to hold him. She likes babies. A lot. And she likes me, too, so I like her, even if she is a baby-hog." Colm hurried to the other side of the room and intercepted Jamie before Mrs. Keller, aka the baby-hog, got him.

Seth turned away from his conversation with his sisters and said, "And that whirlwind was Colm. He will be very careful with Jamie."

"Your brother gave me a nod that basically said the same thing. So tell me, how is he part of the family?"

"Colm works at Keller's Market. It's the family business. When my father retired, Zac started running it. The store works with a lot of Whedon's school and community programs. Colm was placed through the Sunrise Foundation, who helps special needs people in town. Mom and Dad might not be legally adopting new kids, but they can't seem to help themselves and keep adding to the family anyway."

"Speaking of family…" Laura knew she should leave it alone, but knowing and doing were two very different things. "Are you going to talk to your mom and dad? I've noticed you've visited with everyone except them. And you're as far away from them as you can humanly get and still be in the same room."

As she spoke, Seth's smile faded, and by the time she finished the last sentence he was frowning. "Leave it alone, Laura. My parents and I have an under standing."

"Which is?"

"I come to family functions and they cut me a wide berth."

"But—"

"Our relationship is what it is. We've all come to accept that, so it's fine." His tone brooked no argument.

She started to say, *Seth if you ever need to talk, I'm here,* but she didn't get any further than, "Seth—"

"Leave it." It wasn't his tone that said let it go, it was his body language. Tense and stiff, so unlike the normally easygoing man she'd come to know.

"If you change your mind and want to talk—" was all the further she got as he cut her off again with a flat, "I don't and I won't."

She saw his mother head their way with Jamie, and Seth got up and moved down the table to be next to his brother—she searched for the name. Dom.

"I believe this belongs to you." Mrs. Keller handed the baby back to her.

Laura took him into her arms and realized how right he felt there. She'd been so nervous, and now, she felt almost naked without him. "Thanks, Mrs. Keller."

"He's a good baby."

"He is—as long as he's being held. I'll confess, this is the first meal since he was born that I've managed to eat without juggling him, too."

"Well, any time you need an extra pair of hands, you can call on the Kellers. I'll confess, I've passed my love of babies and kids on to my kids. Every one of them is a baby magnet."

"I saw that."

"So, you and Seth are...friends?"

Laura heard the innuendo in those few words. "Yes, ma'am. My fiancé, Jamie's father, was a cop, too. I know you read about cops and their brotherhood in books and things like that, but I didn't really get it. Even when I was planning our wedding, I didn't get it. They have a fierce loyalty to each other, and to each other's families. Even though Jay and I didn't make it to the wedding..." Her voice hitched, and she took a deep breath to regain control. "Jay's group have dropped off home-cooked meals, shoveled when necessary and every Thursday, someone drags the trash cans to the curb and back. They look after me, no matter how much I protest."

"Did Seth and Jay work together?" Mrs. Keller asked.

"No, ma'am. Seth barely knew Jay. I met him when I went to the station because of one of my students. We sort of banded together to help her, and he's stuck around ever since."

"But just as friends." It was a statement, but Mrs. Keller managed to hint at a question.

"Yes," Laura assured her. "He was there the night Jamie was born. I don't think I could have done it without him."

"He was there when you gave birth?" Seth's mom's expression wasn't one of surprise, but rather shock.

"Yes." Wishing she hadn't mentioned it, and hoping to keep his mom from getting the wrong idea, Laura hastily added, "It's not as if we planned it."

"I wouldn't have thought he'd have been able to do that," Mrs. Keller mused.

"I didn't, either. He shouldn't have stayed, but as you probably know, Seth doesn't always listen. He had to be thinking about—"

Mrs. Keller interrupted. "He told you about Allie and the babies?"

"Yes. And the fact that he stayed shows me what kind of man he is—just what kind of man you raised."

Mrs. Keller's smile stretched from ear to ear. "Seth has always had a deep need to protect and help people. I think that's why he went into law enforcement. When May was little, she was a wild child. Always running off and exploring. Seth is four years older, and he appointed himself her guardian. One day, a few months after she came to live with us, she got mad that I told her to clean her room and she packed her bag to run away. Seth followed her all the way downtown and coaxed her into the burger joint. He knew they didn't have any money to pay for their meals, but he ordered them burgers and shakes anyway. Then he told his sister they'd have to either wash dishes to pay for the meals, or call me to come get them and pay, which I did. Then he offered to help her clean her room. And Seth at that age was allergic to cleaning."

"Even then he took care of people."

"Even then." Her voice sounded watery.

"Mrs. Keller?"

"I miss his trust. He was so angry with us when we didn't support his marriage to Allie. Even though they were obviously meant for each other. But we got along, and we admitted we were wrong and apologized. We were rebuilding a relationship, and Allie was really pushing for it. She wanted her children—their children—to know us, to be a part of our lives. And then she died, and..." She nodded at her son on the opposite side of the room. "He's still upset. We just couldn't seem to find the right words to make it better."

Mrs. Keller wiped at her eyes. "And saying all that to you was highly inappropriate. I'm sorry. And I'm glad Seth brought you."

"I'm glad, too, ma'am."

"He looks like he'd like to come back over, and probably won't if I'm here, so I'm going to make myself scarce. I hope we see you again soon, Laura. And I'm not just saying that in order to get a new baby fix."

Laura laughed. "Thank you, Mrs. Keller."

Mrs. Keller moved to sit next to Eli and Zac, scooping up their son...Johnny. Yes, that was his name.

Seth reclaimed his seat. "So, what did my mother want?"

"She introduced herself and said hi." Laura didn't want to let it end there, so she added, "She misses you. Not that you're not here, obviously, but she feels your distance."

He didn't respond. Didn't say anything. Although his expression told her that this was not a topic he cared to discuss. "And on that note, I think it's time I get this little guy home to bed."

"Listen, Laura, I didn't mean—"

"No, it's okay, Seth. It really is time to go home. Jamie's not used to parties."

"I'll walk you out."

Laura bundled up the baby, got ready herself and thanked everyone again for including her. "And, Cecily, congrats on the game. I heard you won...almost single-handedly."

Cessy laughed and scoffed. "We're really a team—we have each other's backs."

Laura wasn't sure if Cessy was talking about the family or her basketball team, but she smiled.

Seth took Jamie's carrier and escorted her to her car.

"Your family seems very nice."

"They are," was his short response.

Laura knew she'd pushed too much about his parents. "Tonight was fun. I think I needed that."

"I didn't have a chance to ask, how are things with JT?"

"They're progressing. I gave her a test that Kaelee, our special service teacher, gave me. I don't think it's a learning disability. Neither does Kaelee. JT and her mom moved around a lot when she was younger. She went to four different grade schools. That's a lot of transition. A lot of moving from one curriculum to another. I think it's more gaps in her education than learning disability. The trick is to fill in the gaps."

"If there's anything I can do, let me know," he offered in his serious tough-guy voice. Softening his tone, he said, "I'm off Wednesday night. We could get together?"

"Seth, I don't want you to feel like you have to babysit me. Your mom seemed surprised that you were comfortable..." She tried to search for the right word. "Being my friend. And I know you say it's not because of the chief, but I don't want to be anyone's obligation."

"You're not an obligation, at least not more than any other friend would be. I mean, if I were sick and needed a ride to the hospital, would you do it?"

She nodded. "Yes, of course, but—"

"How about if I got tossed in jail and needed someone to make my bail?"

She laughed because the idea of Seth doing anything to warrant being in jail was funny. "Sure, I'd find your bail money."

"So ask yourself, if I, your friend, needed to perhaps visit with you next week, can you say no? You should indulge me, because we're friends, and that's what friends do."

"You know, there's a chance you should have been a lawyer instead of a cop. You're very persuasive."

"Some of my best friends are lawyers. And judges. I had to learn to argue and hold my own, or they'd have done me in by now."

He opened the back passenger door for her, and she snapped Jamie's carrier into its base.

He shut the door and opened her driver's door. She stood on tiptoe and kissed his cheek.

Seth recalled the spot where Laura had kissed him. It didn't have to mean anything more than he wanted it to mean.

Looking at her standing there, so vulnerable, he realized he wanted it to mean more than something safe.

He knew his family was still inside Joe Root's, but despite knowing they would always be there for him, he'd felt alone—totally alone—since Allie died. Until now. Until Laura.

Without overanalyzing what he was about to do, he leaned down and kissed her full on the lips. It wasn't just some light peck that she would be able to write off as friendship. It was a kiss full of hunger. Not just desire, though that was there, but a need to feel connected. And he found that here with Laura as she deepened the kiss.

Jamie squawked in the backseat, bringing them both back to reality.

"Seth, I..." Laura seemed stricken as she climbed into the driver's seat and said, "I'll talk to you soon," before shutting the door.

Seth watched as she pulled away.

What the hell had he done now?

BY THE TIME MONDAY ROLLED around, Laura was at her wit's end.

Seth Keller had kissed her. Not some platonic, hey-we're-friends sort of kiss, but a full-out plundering that had left her knees weak.

She'd wanted him.

And the guilt that followed that confession ate at her.

She loved Jay. Truly loved him heart and soul. She'd planned to marry him and build a life with him. She'd given birth to his son.

Then she'd kissed Seth Keller.

What kind of woman did that make her?

Seth called, but she'd let the machine pick up. She didn't know what to say to him.

She was relieved when JT arrived.

She thought she was managing to behave normally, as if she was plain old Laura Watson, mother and teacher, not Laura Watson, woman who went around kissing other men. At least she thought she was managing it until she walked JT to the door after the lesson and the girl asked, "You okay?"

"Why, sure I am," she replied as brightly as possible.

JT didn't look as if she believed her. As a matter of fact, her disbelief was evident. "You should probably try to get some sleep when Jamie takes a nap."

Sleep? What was that? Every time she shut her eyes she dreamed of Jay, or of Seth.

She wasn't sure which dreams left her feeling more guilty.

"Really, get some sleep," JT reiterated as the girl's mother honked her horn.

Laura shut the door and let her happy facade go.

She should call Seth and tell him thank you for everything, but no, thank you. She didn't need him. She—

The doorbell rang, interrupting her internal conversation.

Laura scanned the counter, but didn't see any forgotten books. She wondered what JT had left behind as she picked up Jamie from his baby seat and headed to the door. She stopped a moment as she realized how easily she'd managed it. No hesitation. No worry about dropping him or picking him up wrong.

That was progress.

Every day she was feeling more comfortable with the idea of being a mom.

Laura opened the door to find Eli Keller and a woman she'd never met, standing on her porch.

"Great. You're here." As if an afterthought, she added, "Hi, Laura. This is my friend, Angelina Tucker."

"Just Tucker, please." Tucker was dressed in paint-splattered jeans with holes in the knees, and a sweatshirt that proclaimed, *Tucker's Garage, We Fix 'Em & Paint 'Em Better Than Anyone Else.* The sweatshirt's hood was pulled over her head, but brown curls escaped the sides. The sweatshirt didn't look nearly warm enough for the bitter cold afternoon.

"Please, come in, before you freeze," Laura encouraged them.

Eli turned to Tucker. "See, told you that a sweatshirt isn't a coat, and you were going to freeze."

"I'm fine," Tucker said. "My dad would say that Tucker blood is as thick as mud. We don't get cold. Not like Eli here. She's always freezing. She says you're a teacher, too. I think part of teacher's college curriculum is Worrying 101."

"Maybe," Eli said, laughing at her friend. "Hang on a second, Laura, while we get the stuff from the car."

"Stuff?" Laura asked.

"Uh-huh, stuff."

Eli and Tucker were back at her door a moment later each carrying a big box. "Can you point us to the kitchen?" Eli asked as she kicked off her cute dressy black boots at the same time Tucker kicked off brown work boots.

Laura shut the door. What on earth were they doing here? She simply pointed and said, "Down that way," as she wondered what was going on.

"I was concerned that you wouldn't be here," Eli said, "and we'd have to leave the boxes outside. I mean, it's cold enough, but still."

Laura followed in her wake. "Eli, don't get me wrong. It's lovely seeing you, but do you mind telling me what you're up to?"

"Well, it's not really me. Okay, so some of it's me, but the rest is the Kellers. Yes, my friend, you've been Kellerized."

Laura couldn't help laughing. "Kellerized?"

Tucker snorted and set her box on the counter. "That's right. Once the Kellers decide that you're one of them, there's no escaping. They've adopted me and my son, Bart. I met them through Eli and they just kept us. We'd have been to Cessy's basketball game if my Dad hadn't been sick."

Eli plopped her box on the counter. "Tucker's right. Zac's mom decreed that a new mom shouldn't cook, and called in the troops. There are enough frozen dinners in here to last until Jamie's a year old. She had me check with

167

Seth who said you had a freezer. Please let him be right when he said yes."

"It *was* fairly empty. Then Jay's buddies sent over meals and now this? I may not be able to close it."

"Not everything is for the freezer. Mom—Deborah—sent you packets of snacks. Cut up veggies and cheese. I'm supposed to remind you that since you're nursing you're still eating for two and you need to be sure to get plenty of vegetables and calcium."

"I put individual slices of lasagna in containers and there's some chicken soup stock." Tucker handed her an index card. "Here's the recipe for homemade noodles. It takes a few minutes, but it's fast and so good, if I do say so myself."

"You should," Eli assured her. To Laura she said, "Tucker's soup and lasagna are fantastic."

"Notice Eli qualified my cooking. The soup and lasagna are good. It's just the rest of my cooking that's suspect. But I figure, if you have two dishes you can make without sending people to the hospital, you're doing good."

"And this one." Eli pulled a plastic baggie from the top of the box. "That's from Colm. He said that Anna says his peanut butter and bananas are the best, but bananas get mushy, so he made you peanut butter and jelly. And he added that it's on brown bread and Anna says that's better than white bread. And there's an

168

apple from him. Green. He says those are better than red."

Laura took the bagged sandwich. "Oh, that's so sweet."

"That's Colm. Sweet."

"Not him. All of you." Laura could feel the tears welling up in her eyes. "I don't know how to thank you."

Nor could she explain how she knew they were friends when she'd only talked to Eli on a few occasions, and this was the first time she'd met Tucker. Yet she simply knew it was so.

"Laura, are you all right?"

"Yes. No. I don't know. I've felt so alone since Jay died." As she said the words, a bittersweet yearning filled her, not the stab of pain she usually had. "But over and over, people remind me that I'm not. I have old friends and now new ones. This isn't how I planned things, but the universe keeps reminding me, with no subtlety whatsoever, that people do care."

Eli stopped unpacking the box and leaned over and took Laura's hand. "Life tends to throw us all for a loop sometimes. My loop came in my forties, when I was better able to cope with it. Tucker didn't have the luxury of time when her life was tossed head over heels."

"I was still in high school and found out I was pregnant. I didn't have a mom, so it was tough. But luckily, this teacher took me under her wing."

Eli blushed. "And in so doing, that teacher gained a great friend. The point is, Laura, we all went through—go through—rough patches, and there was and is pain, but..." She paused a moment and said, "My life isn't anything close to what I thought it would be. But it's good. It's special. And despite the pain I went through getting here, I'm happy with where I am."

"And I don't think any kid dreams of being a teen parent, but I don't know where I'd be without Bart. He's the best thing I've ever done," Tucker said. "What we're saying is, life changes unexpectedly. And when it does, you need people in your corner. Now that you've been Kellerized, you have that all over the place."

"I think being Kellerized is the best thing that's happened to me in a long time. I so appreciate what you've said and done today. Both of you. I'll call Seth's mom and thank her."

"You can call any of us, anytime." Eli and Tucker started packing the foil-covered and freezer-bagged food in the freezer. Eli stopped and looked at the pictures on the door. "Your family?"

"I have more formal pictures in the living room, but I like the candid shots more. That's my mom and dad. They were in college in that one." Two young coeds hung from a low tree branch. Her mom's hair was so long it brushed the ground. And her dad's glasses were falling from his head onto his forehead. "And that's Jay and me on the beach. We asked this older couple to take the picture with the sunset behind us."

Eli reached out and touched the plastic-covered photo. "He looks like he was a nice man."

Tucker nodded.

"He was." Was. No longer is. That past tense thing came easier now. It still hurt, but not as much. And it should hurt. She longed for the pain. It was a familiar friend. The guilt she kept experiencing now, wasn't.

"It's good you and Jay's family have Jamie. Jay gets to live on through his son." Eli finished loading up the freezer. "May I?"

Laura nodded and handed her the baby.

Eli cradled him. "He's a lucky boy. He has so many people who love him."

"My turn," Tucker said.

Eli handed the baby to her friend who took the baby with a casual ease. She cradled Jamie up against her loose sweatshirt.

"Speaking of lucky and babies, I have news." Excitement filled Eli's voice. "Big news."

Laura was about to ask what news, when Eli burst out, "We're having a baby. Well, not really, but we're getting one. Although getting sounds wrong. It doesn't matter. We're adopting a daughter and she's coming home soon."

"Excuse Eli." Tucker still cradled Jamie, who looked utterly content. "She has problems forming coherent sentences when she gets excited."

"You know you're excited, too, Tuck."

"Yeah, but I can still talk."

Eli laughed, then turned to Laura. "My daughter's name is Ebony, but she told me she's Ebi, except when she's in trouble, then her foster mother calls her Ebony, so she doesn't like Ebony. She's so smart and funny. She told me she knows all about being a big sister, so Johnny's lucky to get her. I told her we were all lucky to get her."

And at that, the terminally cheerful Eli Keller burst into tears. "She told me that our names almost match. She read my name on the social worker's chart. Ebi and Eli. I broke down then, too." Eli was crying so hard she stopped talking.

Tucker rolled her eyes, but Laura could see she was touched as she found a tissue for Eli.

Eli mopped her tears and said, "Cessy—Seth's youngest sister—wrote this essay at school about being teased because she didn't match Mom."

"The Keller family does have a sort of United Nations feel," Laura said.

"Yes. The teacher sent Mom the essay and she read it out loud my first Keller Christmas, much to Cessy's embarrassment. Laura, that essay...you'll have to read it next time you go over. Mom's got it framed. Cessy ended up taking her whole family in for show-and-tell and informing her classmates that none of them match on the outside. They have different colored skin and hair. But they match on the inside, that they love each other and that's what matters." Eli sniffed. "That's what I told Ebony. That our names almost match, and that's nice, but that's not what matters the most. That we match on the inside because we're a family. She's been my family since the day she was born—she just didn't know it yet. We've been looking for her for a long time, and now we've found her and she's ours."

Eli sniffled. "That's what I need you to understand. Before I got pregnant, I knew where I thought my life was going, but nothing worked out that way. Everything is different. And as our friend Colm would say—different is just different—"

"And that can be very special," Laura finished.

Eli shot Laura a smile that Laura recognized. It was the same smile she used when a student finally got a concept.

"Now, before I go," Eli said, "I'm inviting you to Ebi's Homecoming Day. I don't have an exact date yet from the social worker, but whatever day it's going to be, I'd like you to be there."

"You might as well say yes right off the bat, Laura. Once you've been Kellerized, there's no way out. They'll simply hunt you down. Tell her what a Homecoming is," Tucker commanded.

"Whenever the kids arrived at Mom and Dad's, that's their Homecoming—capitalized, like Christmas. Those children weren't simply adopted...they came home. We're going to carry on the tradition with Ebony. We want everyone, including you and Jamie, to be a part of welcoming our daughter home."

Laura didn't want to go. She wanted to put as much distance between herself and Seth, and conversely, she wanted to be with him as much as possible. How could someone have such warring feelings? "Thank you, but—"

She looked at Eli's obvious excitement and found herself saying, "Thank you. I'd love to be a part of Ebony's Homecoming."

"I'll call Seth and get you both the details." Eli put a hand on Laura's shoulder. "I know this is a difficult time. Remember you have friends. You call if I can do anything."

"You can call me, too, but, unless you have a car that needs fixing or specialty painting, I'm not sure how much use I'll be."

"Don't listen to her," Eli said. "She's very handy."

Tucker handed the baby back to Laura.

"I'll tell you, Tucker, if I can learn to handle a baby with the ease that you do, I'll consider myself very handy."

"That's not tough. Just imagine you're cradling a piston and gently placing it in the engine head and you'll have it."

Laura laughed. "I don't know what that is."

"Eggs," Eli explained. "Babies are like hard-boiled eggs. They require care, but they're tougher than you think they are."

"Now that, I get. Thanks. And, Eli, congratulations again."

"Thanks. My daughter may be home in time for Christmas. That'll be something else to celebrate."

Laura saw them out and felt as if she'd been thrust into the center of an emotional whirlwind. She couldn't really sort through all of it.

When she was teaching Art History, she told the kids if they could finish a lesson and have one take-away, one impression or fact, she'd be happy. Well, though she still felt breathless from the visit, she had her take-away, Colm's phrase about different being special.

Her life was different, but she didn't have to look any further than her son to find some special. She'd known that and held on to that throughout her pregnancy.

Maybe it was now time to start looking around and seeing what other special gifts life had to offer her.

CHAPTER NINE

LAURA BELTED OUT THE CHORUS of a popular tune.

Something had changed since Eli and Tucker's visit two and a half weeks ago. She felt lighter. Happier. And when she was happy, she sang. Badly. Loudly. And with a great deal of gusto.

JT looked up from her math book on the coffee table and laughed. "Trying out for *American Idol,* Ms. Watson?"

She stopped. "Sorry, I didn't mean to sing that out loud." She was sitting on the floor across from JT. Jamie was on his stomach on the floor next to her, studying a stuffed zebra. He could raise his head now.

The book said to make sure he spent time on his tummy each day. It would strengthen his neck, and that soon he'd start doing more than raising his head. He'd be raising his whole torso, then rolling over. Then the world would be his oyster.

"Sometimes happiness spills out." It had been a while since she was so happy that she'd ended up singing. She smiled at the memory of

Jay's teasing—memories that made her smile rather than cry. "I'd like to say being caught by you was the most embarrassing thing that's ever happened to me, but it's not even close. Once, I went to a teacher's conference at a hotel. I was getting ready for the evening and jamming—"

"Jamming?" JT teased.

Laura tried to look indignant. "What, jamming isn't a hip word anymore?"

JT shook her head with what Laura assumed was pity. "Ms. Watson, *hip* isn't a hip word anymore."

Part of Laura's happiness stemmed from JT's progress. JT had brought home an English test— a C-. For JT, that was an improvement. They hadn't worked together that long. By the end of the year, Laura hoped that JT would have a C average.

Feeling overwhelmingly gleeful, Laura continued their "hip" banter. "Well, I'm a mom now and I don't have to be hip. I shouldn't even try to be hip. I mean, a hip mom is a huge embarrassment to a child."

JT shook her head again. "I don't think Jamie has to worry about your hipness." She snorted. "Finish your story. You were at a conference and in a hotel room...?"

Laura ignored JT's rip and continued, "I was in the hotel room by myself, singing as I got ready to meet friends for dinner—friends in the room next to mine. When I went into the hall and met them, they asked what radio station I'd been listening to. I was singing so loudly they'd heard me through the wall." She remembered Pam and Barb's laughter.

"You must have sounded good." JT laughed.

Laura shook her head. "That's what they said, but you heard me. So, I'm sure you'll agree that while I sound very nice through a wall, I'm not quite ready for the *American Idol* competition."

"You're too old to be on *American Idol,* anyway. They have age limits."

"Ouch." Laura and Jay used to joke that they'd be in their mid-twenties until they hit twenty-nine, only then would they admit to being in their late twenties. She smiled at that memory, too. "Go ahead, call me old. I refuse to let you dim my happiness. Today's Jamie's one month birthday. And it occurred to me that a year ago today, I wasn't pregnant yet."

Suddenly, on the heels of that realization came the thought that a year ago, Jay was here, getting ready for Christmas with her, and her bubble of happiness fizzled.

Right after Jay had died, the pain had been constant. Unremitting. Now, there were periods of time she forgot. Not forgot Jay, but forgot the pain. And because she went for times without it, when it did hit, it could buckle her knees.

"You okay?" JT reached out and took her hand. Her short, black fingernails seemed incongruent with the gentleness of her touch.

"Yes. Sure." But she wasn't—not really. She noticed that she'd been happy for hours.

Jay was gone, and she'd kissed Seth Keller two weeks ago. She was pretty sure he felt as bad about that kiss as she did. Neither she nor Seth had mentioned the kiss, and she planned to keep it that way. What did that say about her love?

"So, what about next week?" JT asked. "I mean, we have a half day of school on Monday, then we're off until after the New Year. I don't know if you still want to get together, or not."

"What do you want? I mean, you certainly deserve time off if you want it." Laura didn't relish the quiet afternoons. She missed teaching, and helping JT filled that void.

Yet it was more than fulfilling her need to work. She felt a special bond with JT.

"I kinda would like to keep working, but I wasn't sure if you did. I mean it's almost Christmas."

Laura picked up one of Jamie's blankets and folded it. "JT, I'm here and would love to keep working, if that's what you want."

JT grinned, as if relieved. "Sounds good."

A horn sounded in the driveway. "That's my mom. Gotta go." JT gathered all her books and stuffed them in her bag. "See you tomorrow, Ms. Watson."

"See you then."

After JT had gone, the house seemed quiet. Too quiet. Her happy singing from earlier was gone, as well.

Jamie fussed, so Laura picked him up and they sat in the rocker. Nursing him now was second nature. And suddenly the silence wasn't so profound.

Laura started to hum the song Seth had sung to Jamie. She glanced at the clock. Seth was running late, but he'd be here soon. He had called to say he was stopping over today, if that was okay. It shouldn't be. She shouldn't be happy at the thought of seeing him. She was, and the fact that she was brought on a new wave of guilt. What did she want to do about Seth Keller?

They'd fallen into an easy routine. Laura and Jamie had quiet days together until JT arrived around three-fifteen. They spent the first hour or so on reading. Laura had made flashcards with basic sight words and every day, she added new words to them. When they reached an unfamiliar word, she helped JT sound it out. *Cavern. Mechanics.*

JT was still frustrated on occasion, but she was feeling better about herself. And Laura was thrilled with the speed in which she learned.

After flashcards and reading, they worked on JT's homework assignments.

In November, Seth had been on second shift. This month, he was on first and finished up at work between three and four, depending on the day. Most nights he came over and spent the evening. They ate together, watched television together. Occasionally, they went out somewhere and took Jamie.

It was nice. Comfortable even. She'd started to rely on Seth. Most of the time she didn't think about it, but now, nursing Jamie in the quiet house, she wondered if she'd become too reliant on him.

She was still pondering that question when Seth bounded through the front door. "Sorry. It snowed more than I thought and traffic's brutal." Then he stopped and sniffed. "Something smells good."

"I've got some of Tucker's soup in the Crock-Pot."

They ate, played with Jamie and...did things that any normal couple would do on a winter's evening.

Only they weren't a couple.

They were friends. Friends who spent more time together than apart. Friends who'd shared a kiss that had changed everything. Laura wondered again if she was growing too dependent on Seth.

"About Christmas..." Seth began.

Laura looked up but didn't say anything, mainly because she didn't know what to say.

"My mother called with invitations for both of us. Zac and Eli got word that they can bring Ebi home the day before Christmas Eve. It's her Homecoming and you're invited." He kept plowing through his invitations. "And there's Christmas dinner. You're invited to that, too."

Laura didn't mind being Kellerized. To be honest, it was a very lovely thing. But she wasn't sure she could spend Christmas with them. "Christmas is a time for family, Seth."

"You and Jamie are my family. Sort of. I'd like to spend the holidays with you, but if you don't want—"

His comments struck her as too much. "Seth, what exactly is our relationship? We're not a couple. I don't know—"

He cut off her sentence by kissing her. Not some platonic buss on the cheek, or even a friendly kiss on the lips.

This one spoke of attraction and a hunger that Laura suddenly felt keenly. Or maybe it wasn't that sudden. Maybe she hadn't wanted to acknowledge that she'd felt something more than friendship for Seth for a while. It had been so long since she'd been held like this. Her lips joined to his. A tentative exploration that quickly deepened into something more.

She twined her arms around his neck, his arms wrapped around her waist. The kiss went on and on, his hands stroking her back, pulling her closer. She touched his short stubbly hair that was surprisingly soft.

For the first time in so long, Laura felt connected to someone. She felt wanted and cherished.

It felt good.

She hadn't been held like this since...Jay.

Jay.

She hadn't thought about Jay as she'd kissed Seth. That realization made her feel as if she'd cheated. It was crazy, and she knew it. Jay was gone. But she still felt as if she'd betrayed him. She pulled away from Seth. "I can't do this."

"I understand."

She nodded, not surprised in the least that Seth would.

"Everyone says the person you lost would want you to be happy, but—"

"But. Yes, there's that great big *but*. I do know Jay wouldn't begrudge me happiness, just like I wouldn't have begrudged it to him, *but* I can't. Not yet. I'm not sure when." Laura reached out and took his hand. "You know, for me to say I can't because of baggage sounds so utterly boring. I've read a lot of romances. The characters have these huge external conflicts to keep them apart. He's a prince, she's a serf. She's a defense attorney—"

"And he's the prosecution."

"He's a carnivore, she's a vegan."

"He's a cop and she's...?"

"An international art thief." He laughed, which had been her intent. She added, "A stymied artist who tried teaching, but now has turned to stealing works of art. You know what they say? Those who can't teach...or steal."

They both laughed together for a few minutes, and finally Seth said, "This is where one of us should say, another time, another place."

"That needed to be said, because it's true. You've become my best friend, Seth."

"And you, mine." He squeezed her hand. "I don't want to lose your friendship because of a few kisses."

"So, we set aside the attraction and be each other's friend. We've got JT and Jamie. That's enough for now. The rest—well, it's not something big and external keeping us apart, but I can't put it aside." Laura knew it would be easier if they were a cop and an art thief. You could stop being an art thief, but she wasn't sure how to stop loving Jay.

"Star-crossed, like Romeo and Juliet," he murmured.

Laura nodded. "If we were a Capulet and a Montague, then we'd have a great external conflict. But alas, you're a Keller and I'm a Watson...and worse still, I like you. I don't want to lose you."

He thrust out his hand. "Friends?"

"Friends."

For a moment, he looked as if he was going to say something more on the subject, but in the end he simply picked up their pre-kiss conversation. "So, about Mom's invites? I'd love to have you there. You know that things are strained with my parents."

"Would you like to talk about it?" Talking about his family wasn't something Seth did, but she hoped things had changed enough for him to reconsider.

"No." His monosyllabic response was definitely to the point.

Laura didn't know what to say, but Seth saved her from trying to find something by continuing, as if she'd never asked about his family. "If you came it would be easier. Having a friend by my side."

"I'll come to Ebony's Homecoming. I couldn't miss that. But Christmas..." She paused, needing him to understand. "I really need to do this one on my own. Just me and Jamie. I need to mourn Jay and figure out how to start this new year without him. Do you understand?"

"Yes. Better than most. The first Christmas after I lost Allie, I went to Atlantic City."

"To gamble?" Seth didn't seem like someone who'd lose himself in games of chance, but everyone dealt with loss in their own way.

She wondered what her way was?

"No, not gambling. I thought maybe, but no. I ended up sitting on the boardwalk and remembering my last Christmas with Allie. It's amazing how much can change in a period of months. I needed that holiday on my own to...well, process it all. So, I'll tell Mom we're on for Ebony's Homecoming, but not for Christmas."

"You should go to Christmas with your family, Seth. I'm not going to nag you about your parents and insist you talk to me about it, but you ought to be with them."

He was quiet a moment, then nodded. "Maybe. Things have changed with us...been better. We'll see." He stood. "And speaking of going, I'd better go."

She didn't get up to show him out. "I'll see you tomorrow," was all she said.

She sat with Jamie long after the baby had fallen asleep, thinking about kissing Seth. It felt right, and the fact that it did felt oh-so-wrong.

Friends. They'd be friends.

SETH COULD HAVE KICKED himself. He'd pushed Laura too hard too fast.

It had been so long since he'd wanted anyone. To be honest, he wasn't sure he'd ever wanted anyone the way he wanted Laura.

With Allie there had been a gentle familiarity. They'd grown up together. He knew everything about her. She knew everything about him. And after he lost her, he hadn't opened up and shared himself with another woman.

Until Laura.

And now this...this feeling for her. He wasn't sure how to think of it, and he refused to label it. But it was there and it was growing.

Now, the question was, what to do about it?

And the only answer was, he'd simply be her friend. For now.

The type of friendship he was developing with Laura was a rare thing. What she'd said was true, they still had JT and now Jamie. And they had genuine concern for each other.

That would have to be enough.

It was either friendship, or losing Laura.

Which means, friendship was his only option, because Laura had become too important—he couldn't lose her.

LAURA HAD WORRIED THAT THINGS would be awkward with Seth after the earth-shattering kiss, but they weren't. At least not on the surface.

But something had altered. It wasn't a distance, which is what she'd feared. If anything, they become closer. It seemed Seth was forever touching her. A friendly pat on the back. Fingers brushing as they handed Jamie off to each other. Platonic good-night kisses on the cheek at the door.

She wasn't sure if the touching was new, or if she was merely more attuned to it. It made her uneasy, but she didn't tell him to stop, because what made her most uneasy was the fact that she welcomed his touch. She felt guilty, yet craved the physical contact. The duality of her feelings confused her. She tried to tell herself it was simple human contact she needed, but she didn't crave it with anyone but Seth.

Laura wanted to back out of the Homecoming celebration at the Keller's, but couldn't find a graceful way to do it, which is why she was driving with Seth down I-79 to Whedon on the night before Christmas Eve. They took her car on the short drive since the car seat was tethered into place.

Laura had gone through Whedon on occasion but hadn't paid much attention. But as they drove through the town all decorated for the holiday season, she thought it was everything a small town should be. There were wreaths on the streetlights that lined the main street, and a large pine in a park in the center of town that was covered in lights.

"Every year the kids at the elementary school make decorations," Seth told her. "There's a big tree lighting ceremony the weekend after Thanksgiving. Last year, they had a fundraiser to buy new LED lights because they use so much less energy."

Seth pulled up in front of a large, rambling-looking house. Electric candles glowed in all the windows. Icicle lights hung from the porch's eaves.

Seth turned off the car, reached over and squeezed her hand gently. He took her into the house. The entryway was crowded with boots. Hooks on the wall couldn't accommodate all the coats, so the overflow was piled on the stair banister.

"Looks like the gang's all here," Seth said. "Every time I turn around, *the gang* is bigger."

Mrs. Keller spotted them.

"Seth, Laura, you're here." Seth picked up Jamie's carrier and stepped neatly behind Laura, as Mrs. Keller pulled her into a hug. She saw the flash of sadness in Mrs. Keller's eyes, but then it was gone and she was smiling as she led Laura into the packed living room. "We're so glad you and Jamie could join us. Come with me."

The living room was decorated to the nth degree. Fortunately, for the Kellers it was big enough to hold all their friends *and* the decorations. The tree in the far corner was so big that the angel on the top bumped against the ceiling. A menorah sat on the fireplace mantel. Candles, evergreen boughs, sprigs of holly and other signs of the season decorated every possible surface. It was chaotic and...well, perfect. People spilled from the living room into the equally decorated dining room. Laura recognized most of Seth's family this time and their friends. Colm, Tucker, Ariel...

"Laura, Seth, you're here," Eli cried as Laura and Seth entered the room. She hurried toward them and enveloped them both in a hug. "I'm so glad. I'd like you to meet my daughter, Ebony."

Zac followed behind Eli, a little girl's hand firmly clasping his. "Ebony, this is my brother Seth," he said. "Your uncle Seth now. And this is his friend, Ms. Watson."

"I sure got a lot of uncles and aunts," Ebony said. "But I don't got no other Ms. Watsons."

Laura knelt down to the girl's eye-level. She was very petite. Her complexion was a light-brown color, her long, dark hair was gathered into a bow. When she looked at Laura, her eyes were a startling green. "Ebony, all these uncles and aunts mean you are a very lucky girl. You can call me Laura, if you like."

Ebony nudged the carrier that Seth had set down between them. "You've got a baby in there?"

Laura nodded, pulled back the blanket and took her son out of his seat. "This is Jamie."

Ebony pushed Jamie's hat aside. "Aw, he's cute. I like babies. We had 'em at the foster home, and now I got a baby brother of my own. I'm gonna help my new mom and dad with him."

"I'm sure you'll be a great big sister," Laura assured her.

Ebony nodded, as if that was a certainty, then hurried back into the sea of Kellers.

Laura smiled at the two new beaming parents. "She's beautiful, Zac and Eli."

"Yes, she is," Eli agreed.

"Oh, here we go," Zac said.

Mr. and Mrs. Keller carried trays of fluted drinks and handed them out. "A toast," Mr. Keller said. "To our new granddaughter. Ebony, we're very happy to celebrate your Homecoming." The big burly man gave his wife a tender, beseeching look as if he'd used up all the words at his disposal and counted on her to rescue him.

May called out, "Oh, don't worry, Dad, I'm sure Mom's got something to add."

Cessy called out, "But no reading things your children wrote today, okay, Mom?"

Mrs. Keller shook her head with obvious mock-exasperation. "Are you children trying to say I talk too much?"

"No, Mom," Dom said. "We figure you talk enough to fill in the blanks for Dad, is all."

"And Dad has lots of blanks," Layla added.

Laura looked at Mrs. Keller being teased by her family with such love and humor and before Seth's mother said another word, Laura felt the tears begin to pool in her eyes.

"We Kellers have always loved celebrations. Homecomings are my favorite. From the time a child walks into my home, they're mine. The missing part of the family. So, Homecomings are just that. A day when we bring that missing piece of our family home where they belong. And that is why they're the best celebrations. And tonight, we're happy to welcome Ebony home where she's always belonged."

Mrs. Keller leaned down to her new granddaughter and said, "Welcome home, Ebony."

"Welcome home," everyone else echoed, and Laura noted that she wasn't the only one with tears in her eyes as she watched Ebony being hugged by new family member after new family member.

Laura listened to the murmur of voices, welcoming Ebony into the family. "Ah, another Homecoming," Seth said to Laura. "My mother would have a holiday every week if she could."

"And with so many children she almost does," Dom said. "And then there are all the birthdays, Valentine's, but also Chanukah, Christmas..."

"New Year's," Cessy called out

"St. Patrick's Day," said May.

Zac laughed and added, "Flag Day."

"Any excuse for Mom's cooking is my thought," Dom yelled out.

"Your mother does know how to throw a party. Ebony, welcome home." As Laura watched Ebony bask in her new family's attention, she kept tearing up. The Kellers were what every family should be. When she watched how awkwardly Seth behaved around his parents, she wanted to meddle. More than meddle, she wanted to go shake some sense into him.

If she had people like this in her life—people who loved so easily and completely—she'd never cut herself off from them, no matter what the reason. And out of the blue, she thought of the Martins, but it wasn't the same, she assured herself. They were Jay's family. Jamie's family. Not hers.

"Hey, Laura, did you get my sandwich?" Colm called out, interrupting her thoughts.

"I did, Colm, and it was delicious. Thank you."

"Yeah. Mrs. Keller said everyone needed to feed you and I make those best."

Before she could reply, Colm asked, "Did you get your tree up? Me and my friends, Gilly and

Josh, put ours up. It sort of leans a little, and has a big bare spot, but I like it."

"I'm not sure I'm going to do a tree this year, Colm." She'd considered it, but hadn't been able to make herself go get one.

"Well, maybe you got a menn-thing instead? Some people have those candle things instead of trees. Mrs. Keller, she's got both."

"A menorah. No, I don't have one of those, either."

Colm looked as if he had more to say on the subject, but Seth came over and asked, "Hey, Colm, how're things at work?"

"Good. Did you see Ariel was here with Nora? I'm gonna go get her and Johnny and tell 'em a story. Ya think Ebony wants to hear one, too?"

"I'm sure she does."

Colm hurried off across the room, collecting the kids as he went.

"Thanks," Laura said. "I was being grilled on my Christmas prep, or lack thereof. I think I disappointed Colm."

"Laura, maybe we could—"

Laura didn't hear the rest of what Seth was going to say. His sister May came and swept Laura into the midst of the family.

SETH WATCHED AS LAURA FELL easily into the party for his new niece. The little girl had charmed the family as easily as Laura had.

They both fit.

He wished he still did. It was almost easier when he rarely saw his family. It was easy to forget that he no longer fit in. But now that he spent more time with them, he was reminded at every gathering.

"I'm supposed to come over here and see if you're okay. Subtly," Tucker said. "That's what Eli said—I'm supposed to be subtle. You'd think, after knowing me all these years, Eli would know I don't do subtle well." Tucker plopped on the couch next to him. "So, are you?"

"Am I what?"

"Okay? They figure since I wasn't a real Keller, you'd be more at home telling me."

"I'm fine. You can report back that you got that out of me with all kinds of subtlety."

"Great." Tucker clapped her hands together. "Now that that's done, I wondered if you ever thought about doing something with your truck?"

"Doing what?"

"Well, you being a cop and all, I had this idea of painting a thin blue line on it. Get it. Thin blue line?"

"I get it." The thin blue line represented the camaraderie of police.

"I know sometimes they use pin-striping for something like that, but I'm a freehander all the way, and I think I could do something more. I had this idea..."

Seth hadn't thought about having any painting done on his truck, but Tucker's enthusiasm was contagious, and he found himself agreeing to drop the truck off at the shop sometime soon. They talked cars and then sports, and by the time Tucker left to get some cake, more than an hour had passed.

"Hey, aren't you worried that Laura's going to get jealous, what with you spending all that time immersed in conversation with another woman?" Dom asked as he sat next to Seth. He strategically propped his crutches between the end table and the couch, so they were out of the way of foot traffic. "Laura kept checking you two out."

"Laura's not jealous because we're not...we're just friends."

Dom snorted. "Is that what they're calling it?"

"I—"

"Don't," Dom said. "I'm sorry. I shouldn't have teased you. It's just that the whole family is thrilled that you've found someone. We weren't sure you'd ever get over Allie."

"I won't ever get over her. She'll always be a part of me. That sounded more wussy than I intended, but you know what I mean."

Dom nodded. "I do. And I didn't mean to be flip. What I'm trying to say is that we all like Laura."

"Me, too. As a friend. If you could spread that around."

"Sure. But, Seth, I'm pretty sure I'm one of the least insightful Kellers, and I can see that she's more than a friend. Her and Jamie."

Seth didn't reply and Dom didn't push the issue. His brother might claim he wasn't insightful, but he was. A physical therapist needed to not only be able to push their patients to get better, but they needed to understand what a patient needed. Seth wasn't one of Dom's patients, but he knew his brother was good at his job.

Laura came over to them. "Hi, Dom. Seth. I hate to interrupt, but Jamie's getting fussy. I wondered if you minded leaving."

Seth normally felt a wave of relief when he left a family gathering, but this one seemed easier and though he didn't mind leaving, he wasn't anxious to, either. "Sure, let's get Jamie home."

They said goodbye to everyone, and as Laura dressed Jamie, Ebony came over and tugged at Seth's hand. "Uncle Seth, will you come see me soon? Mom says you sometimes don't come to Christmas, but I said you would this time 'cause it's my first Christmas, and you're my uncle."

There was such a look of complete confidence in her eyes there was nothing for Seth to say, but, "Yes, I'll be here."

"See, Mom, I told you he'd come," Ebony called to her new mother.

"I'm glad," Laura said softly.

Despite feeling awkward sometimes, Seth glanced back at his family and had to admit, so was he.

CHAPTER TEN

LAURA HADN'T DECORATED FOR the holidays. Seth hadn't thought a lot about it until last night when Ebony had looked at him so trustingly and said she'd known he'd show up for Christmas because it was her first one with the family. Well, it was Jamie's first Christmas, too, and he, at the very least, deserved a tree.

It was Christmas Eve, and once Seth finished his shift and changed at the station, he'd head to the Burbules tree lot he always used to go to. He knew just how to handle the tree issue in such a way that Laura couldn't say no.

Half an hour later, he showed up on her porch, tree in hand. He knocked on the door, then let himself in.

"I'll be out in a minute, Seth," she called.

"Take your time, Laura."

Ten minutes later when she walked into the living room, she spotted his purchase and frowned. "Seth, I thought you understood that I didn't want to decorate and why."

"I do, but hear me out. First, this isn't really a Christmas *tree*. It's hardly more than a Christmas branch." The three foot *branch* in question sat lazily in the stand. "Charlie Brown's tree looked practically lush compared to this. And it's Christmas Eve. If I hadn't taken the tree, it would have just been composted. Laura, even if it's Christmas twigs, they deserve their moment to shine." He plugged in the small strand of lights he'd picked up. "Literally shine."

"Seth." She sighed his name, trying to sound exasperated, but he could hear a hint of laughter in it.

"And someday, Jamie will be looking through his baby album and he'll wonder why he didn't have a tree on his first Christmas. You wouldn't deny him that, would you?"

"I can see what you're doing."

"What?" he said with as much innocence as he could muster.

She just shook her head, and Seth knew he'd won. "I got something else, too." He handed her a bag. "My mom collected ornaments for each of us. A new one every Christmas. I thought that might be a nice thing to start for Jamie, as well."

The ornament was a round ball with a baby in a crib embossed with Baby's First Christmas.

Laura smiled. "It's a lovely tradition. Thank you."

Seth didn't ask about other ornaments. Laura's other memories might not be as joyful. He thought it best to let those ghosts of Christmases past rest.

"There's a couple more things in the bag." He extended it to Laura.

She pulled out the heavy thread, package of needles and a bag of popcorn. "You want to get to work?"

After he popped the popcorn, they sat side by side on the couch, stringing popcorn and watching *It's a Wonderful Life.*

Laura seemed happy.

And as far as Seth was concerned, that was enough to make this one of his nicest Christmas Eves in a very long time.

LAURA WOKE UP CHRISTMAS DAY with a sense of hope. It was a perfect morning. It had snowed the night before, just a dusting, but enough to cover the brown road slush with a fresh coat of crystal white. She lit the tree and fingered Jamie's ornament that sat amongst the popcorn.

She'd been afraid Seth was going to ask her to get the rest of her ornaments, but he didn't. Leave it to Seth to understand that those memories might hurt.

Part of her wished she was spending the day with Seth and his family. She'd liked them when she met them at that dinner at Joe Root's, but at Ebony's Homecoming, she'd simply fallen in love with Seth's family and hadn't forgotten wanting to somehow help him find his way back to them.

But as much as she would have liked to have been with them, with Seth, she needed today on her own with Jamie, her memories of Jay and her dreams of what their life might have been.

Jamie still hadn't woken up when, coffee in hand, she pulled out her photo album and took it to the couch in front of the fire. Pictures of their vacation to Gettysburg. Jay standing next to the statue of Strong Vincent, an Erie Civil War hero. They'd had to hunt in a copse of trees to find it.

Pictures of their engagement party. Her and Jay, toasting each other.

Last Christmas, the two of them in front of the fireplace. Jay had set the timer on the camera. It had taken four shots to get their faces in the frame. She'd kept their knees, their torsos and finally the two of them laughing because they weren't sure what they'd get this time. Laughing in front of the fireplace on Christmas. At the moment that photo was taken, the two of them had believed they'd be married by the next Christmas—this Christmas. They'd believed they had an entire life to build together.

She traced his photo with her finger. She'd forgotten him like this. Her memories centered around a hospital bed and the funeral home.

This was Jay.

Hamming for the camera with a statue in Gettysburg. Toasting her, loving her. Laughing.

This was the man she'd tell Jamie about. His father. A man of laughter and love.

She decided that she'd get the photo from last Christmas blown up and framed for Jamie. She pulled it out of the album and stared at it.

For a moment she allowed herself to fantasize that the life they thought they'd have had happened. Once, those fantasies had come so easily, but now, she had to work to imagine the life she'd planned. It was as if her subconscious had finally accepted that Jay was gone, and with him, that imagined future.

She gave up the attempt when Jamie woke up and started crying.

She changed his diaper and sat in the rocker nursing him and as she rocked her son, she realized she didn't need a fantasy when she had Jamie. He made everything better.

When he finished nursing, they moved to the living room. "Merry Christmas, Jamie."

She opened his present for him. A baby play mat. Bright colored toys hung over it, and she tucked Jamie under them and watched as he kicked his feet and batted his hands.

She opened the rest of his gifts and wondered why she'd even bothered wrapping them. She couldn't help but think this was a waste of wrapping paper, and she did her best to be green. In the end, she decided she'd wrapped them for the same reason Seth had brought the tree—this was Jamie's first Christmas.

Three presents remained wrapped under the small tree after Jamie's were opened.

She put Jamie's new Raffi CDs into the player and sang "Baby Beluga" with him. She'd done some student teaching with preschoolers and had fallen in love with the slipper-wearing, bearded, Canadian singer.

It was almost lunchtime when the doorbell rang and startled Laura. She'd planned on having the day to herself. Just her and Jamie. Her family, small though it was, was enough for Christmas.

JT stood on the porch wearing a coat that Laura thought looked much too light for the weather, a backpack and with a present in hand. "JT, I didn't think I'd see you today."

"I can't stay long. Mom's making me go to the new boyfriend's with her. We're going to have a *real family Christmas.*" JT's words dripped with disbelief as she came into the house.

Laura waved at JT's mother in the car, and the woman waved back. "JT, I'm sure—"

"I'm sure, too, Ms. Watson." JT snorted. "Mom promised it would be different this time. Poor guy might believe it, but I know better. He'll be gone before Valentine's."

"JT..."

JT shook her head. "No. Sorry. I didn't come to bitch at you. My mom is...well, she's my mom. I can't change her. But I can change myself. You taught me that." She thrust the package at Laura. "Here."

"Come into the living room," Laura said, carrying her present. Jamie was still on the floor, staring at the baby toys hanging above him.

"Come on, Ms. Watson." JT was excited, that much was evident.

Laura sat on the couch and slowly opened the package. It was a sketch of her cradling Jamie. "Oh, JT, it's beautiful."

"I snapped a picture with my cell phone when you weren't looking and used that for the sketch so it would be a surprise."

It was easy to admire the strong, bold strokes that spoke of a far more mature talent than most high school students. "It's good, JT. Very good."

JT shrugged, but Laura could tell she was pleased with the praise. She got up and took one of the three remaining gifts from under the tree and handed it to JT. "Santa left something here for you, too. Here."

Laura grinned as JT opened the package with great care. She'd have thought the girl would be a ripper, instead, she was a cautious unwrapper.

She held the box of charcoals and huge sketchbook. "Thanks, Ms. Watson." Then she spotted the leather-bound book of O. Henry stories.

"I've always thought that reading a well-bound book was so much more pleasurable than reading a paperback. Jay used to say I was a book snob." She laughed at the memory. "Anyway, check out the story 'The Gift of the Magi' first. It's a classic Christmas story. A woman sells her hair to give her husband a watch fob."

"Watch fob?"

"Before wristwatches they carried watches in their pockets. The watch fob held the watch. And he sold the watch to buy her combs for her hair."

JT was quiet a moment, then said, "Oh. They both gave up something they loved for someone they loved."

Laura was delighted that JT got the gist of the story so quickly. "I loved O. Henry's work when I was younger, and while it's a classic now, the writing isn't too difficult. I thought you could read it and then we could discuss it."

JT hefted the book. "It might take a while."

"JT. That book's been around for years and it's not going anywhere. However long it takes, it takes."

A horn beeped.

"That's my mom. I'd better go. Merry Christmas, Ms. Watson." She took another wrapped gift from her backpack. "Could you leave this one for the lieutenant?"

Laura took the gift. "Sure. I'll put it under the tree."

"See you bright and early Monday."

"See you then."

Laura sat on the couch and studied JT's gift. It was gorgeous. She'd hang it in her room.

She put JT's gift for Seth under the tree and wondered if he'd gone to his family's. She hoped he had. She wondered what she could do to help him mend the rift between him and his parents.

A good first step would be getting him to talk about whatever their problems were.

She was still wondering two hours later when the Martins arrived. Laura knew when she said she wanted a quiet Christmas on her own that she couldn't exclude the Martins. But she wasn't ready for the emotions that flooded her as she opened the door for them. She remembered last year and everything they'd planned together.

This wasn't anything close to what she'd imagined.

The Martins cried in unison, "Merry Christmas, Laura!" But Laura only felt cheated. She didn't say that, though. She merely said, "Merry Christmas." She ushered them into the house. "Please, come in. Jamie's awake and playing with his new Christmas toy. Well, not playing. Staring at it as he goos and kicks his feet, but I think that means he likes it."

Mrs. Martin jiggled a bag filled with gifts. "I couldn't seem to stop."

Mr. Martin patted his wife's back. "The baby now has a wardrobe for the next year at least."

"You know better than that, Jameson," Mrs. Martin scolded. "They grow so fast. Before you know it, Jamie won't let us buy him clothes. He'll need new, hip stuff."

Laura couldn't help but think of her discussion with JT a while back and said, "I've been assured that the word *hip* isn't hip." Laura realized she was joking with the Martins like she would have last year and she felt awkward. She watched as they cooed over the baby. Mrs. Martin offered to let her open Jamie's gifts, but she declined and let them open them for Jamie.

She'd have left them alone with their grandson, but she thought that might seem rude, so she stayed.

"And this is for you," Mrs. Martin said, extending a small gift. "It's from Jay, in a way."

"Jay?" Her fingers trembled as she took the small package.

"My mother left it for him to someday give to his wife," Mrs. Martin explained. "He planned on giving it to you after the wedding, but since he can't I'm doing it for him."

Laura handed the box back. "Really, I can't take it. Maybe you should save it for Jamie's wife someday."

Mrs. Martin didn't take the gift. "Laura, I know things aren't right with us, and I'm hoping someday they will be, but for now, know that this is what Jay wanted."

There was no way to say no to that. She opened the box and found a gold ring with a small sapphire. "He was going to give it to you the night before your wedding so you'd have something blue."

"Oh." She slipped it on her finger. It fit the middle finger on her left hand, sitting next to her engagement ring that she still hadn't managed to take off. She decided today was the day. Later, she'd take it off.

"Thank you." She was relieved she'd thought to get something for Jay's parents. "There's something under the tree for the two of you, too."

She got the package. "It's small, but I thought..." She trailed off. She wasn't sure what had prompted her to dig through her box of lists, but she had. She hoped the Martins liked the framed copy of Jay's Thanksgiving list from last year.

I am thankful for my parents. For my father, who taught me what it is to balance a demanding job with a family and never let either suffer. He taught me exactly what a husband and father should be. And I'm thankful for my mother, who taught me what loving unconditionally meant. That kind of love is a rare thing. And last, but by no means least, I'm thankful for Laura, who believes I can be the kind of man my father is, and loves with the same unconditional heart that my mother does. I'm a lucky man.

She'd framed a picture of the Martins and Jay on the day he'd been sworn in as a police officer. Both men in pressed uniforms flanking a glowing Mrs. Martin. "I thought, for Christmas, you should have something from Jay and this struck me as perfect. He loved and respected you both. I thought remembering that would make this first Christmas without him easier."

Easier. She fingered the ring that felt foreign on her finger. Easier but by no means easy.

For a moment she could almost believe that things were back to the way they'd been last Christmas, but an image of Jay in the hospital and the memory of Mrs. Martin's hurtful words ruined her nostalgia. Mrs. Martin had taken away her ability to honor Jay's last wishes.

Her anger was still there, bubbling beneath the surface. She knew they were hurting, too, and her anger toward them made her feel guilty as well.

It seemed as if her life had become a circle of pain, grief and guilt. She didn't know how to break the cycle. But for today she'd try to set it aside.

She reminded herself that Jay had loved his parents so much, and for his sake, she needed to try harder.

And suddenly, she wanted to do more to ease the pain of their loss. "Mrs. Martin, I wanted to ask if you'd consider watching Jamie on occasion?"

The words came out of her mouth before she'd really thought about them. But watching the Martins look so lovingly at the picture of Jay, watching them interact with Jamie, she knew it was the right thing to do. "There are little things I need to do sometimes that I can't take Jamie to. A haircut, for instance. My hair has started to take on a life of its own. There's no way to juggle a baby at a beauty salon and—"

Mrs. Martin interrupted her, "Oh, Laura, we'd love to watch him. Anytime. For however long you need."

"I can't think of anyone else I'd trust with him." Well, anyone other than Seth.

And she realized that was true. Things might not be right between her and Jay's parents, but she knew that they'd look after Jamie with all the love and care that she did.

"There's one more thing," Mr. Martin, who'd been very quiet, said. "I know Jay took out a life insurance policy in your name the week after he found out you were pregnant. I went with him when he did."

Laura had been shocked to find out about the policy after Jay's funeral. The money was a huge boon. It gave her a financial cushion. They'd planned on Laura taking the rest of the school year off after having the baby, and not returning to school until the next year. Jay's life insurance meant she still could. She'd seriously planned on going back after her maternity leave, but had just talked to the principal about staying home until the start of the next school year. It was up to her, she simply hadn't decided yet.

"Well, the department has a small policy for each officer, too," Mr. Martin continued, "but Jay hadn't changed all his paperwork to your name yet, so it came to us."

"As it should have," she said.

"But we don't need or want it," Mr. Martin said. "So we put it into a college savings program for Jamie."

"Mr. and Mrs. Martin, I don't know what to say."

"Say you'll accept it in the spirit it was given. Not only is it what Jay would have wanted, it's what we want. We love this baby. Not because he's a piece of Jay, but because he's our grandson. Knowing he'll be able to go to college and not worry about it, well that's a gift to ourselves as much as a gift to him."

How could she argue with that? "Thank you."

Mrs. Martin nodded.

Conflicting feelings warred within her. She couldn't sort them out. Fortunately, the Martins let the subject drop. They stayed and visited for another hour, but when Jamie went down for his nap, they got up to leave.

"You make your hair appointment for whenever you want. Let me know and I'll be here," Mrs. Martin promised.

"Do you have anything on your schedule that would make it hard?"

"Laura, there's nothing on my schedule now, or ever, that would take precedence over my grandson and you. Not ever."

Mrs. Martin took a step toward Laura, as if she were going to embrace her, but Laura took a step back, maintaining a distance. "I appreciate that. But it's just a hair appointment. I can make it anytime."

Mrs. Martin reached out and hugged her before Laura could move out of the way. "Thank you for a beautiful Christmas, Laura."

Mr. Martin hugged her as well. It was a bit less all-embracing.

As she waved goodbye to them, she realized something had eased. Their relationship had altered since that day in the hospital, and Laura wasn't sure they'd ever get it back to where it had been, but for the first time she felt optimistic that they'd find some footing and build a new relationship.

Less than a half hour after the Martins left, the doorbell rang again. Laura's heart sped up, knowing it was probably Seth. She should be annoyed that he hadn't listened to her request for a Christmas on her own, but instead, she swung back the door with a smile. "Merry Christmas, Seth."

He didn't reply, but rather scooped her into a hug. This one she didn't pull back from. With her face pressed to his thick winter coat, she could smell a spicy warmness that she'd never be able to define, but that she recognized instantly as his.

"Merry Christmas, Laura."

She ushered him inside. He took off his coat and hung it on a hook, very much at home by now.

"My quiet Christmas hasn't been so very quiet." She told him about JT and the Martins' visit. "JT left you a present."

"I have one for her, too. I'm sorry I missed her." He sat down on the couch. "No Jamie?"

"Still napping. I know he's too little to understand Christmas, but he certainly got caught up in the hustle and bustle of it all. He was awake all morning and went down hard."

She got Seth his gifts and set the small pile on the coffee table in front of him. Seth picked up JT's first. She'd made him a similar sketch of him on the floor playing with Jamie.

Laura reached out to touch it briefly and imagined that it was Jay playing so tenderly with their son. The ring the Martins had given her sparkled next to her engagement ring.

She was hit again with the thought that Jay should be here.

Seth noticed. There was no surprise there— Seth always noticed.

"You okay?" he asked.

She nodded. "It's hard. It's my first Christmas without him."

"I remember my first Christmas without Allie was the worst. You are not alone, even if that's what you said you wanted." He offered her an unrepentant smile. "You'll get through this Christmas and the next one will be easier."

"Promise?" she asked.

Seth took her hand in his and squeezed. "Promise."

They sat like that for a few seconds, or maybe minutes. Laura wasn't sure. She simply knew that Seth being here helped.

He finally broke the silence. "Think about it, next Christmas Jamie will be on the move. Probably tearing all the ornaments off the tree every time you turn your back."

"I should probably invest in some plastic ones. I can hit the after-Christmas sales. I bet Mrs. Martin would watch Jamie for a few hours."

She could see that Seth understood it was a big deal. "You've decided to let them watch Jamie?"

"We're going to try. I know eventually I'll be back at work and I'll have to leave him."

"When is your maternity leave over?"

"I was supposed to go back in February, but I've been talking to the principal about taking off the rest of the year and starting back in the fall. I'm torn between missing my students, and knowing that leaving Jamie will be a hard thing to do." She could feel herself on the verge of tears, so she changed the subject. "How was it at your parents? You did go, right?"

"Yes, I went and it was better. Things have been...easier."

She didn't press, but simply asked, "How was Ebony?"

"She's already a real heartbreaker. She's twisted every male family member around her little finger. She walked up to Dom and tapped one of his braces and asked him about it. He started to give her a watered down medical explanation, and she shook her head and said, 'No, Uncle Dom, you're like Iron Man. A hero.'"

"Iron Man?" Laura asked.

"Comic series, now movies. Robert Downey, Jr.?"

She shook her head.

"Let's just say, it was a compliment. And because she didn't want me feeling bad, she said, police officers were heroes, too, just not as much as Iron Man."

"What did happen to Dom's legs?"

"A spine injury when he was a baby. Before my parents adopted him."

"Speaking of heroes." She retrieved the last wrapped gift under her tree and handed it to him. Seth opened it slowly. It was a framed photo of him holding Jamie minutes after he was born. "I thought the moment should be immortalized. You were my hero that night. I thought I wanted to go it alone, but I needed you. Sort of like today."

"Laura, you'll never be alone. You've got me, Jamie and a host of other people." He studied the picture. "You know, I've been called out to hairy calls, but that day, being there when you gave birth, I was never so scared. And afterward, holding Jamie, I'd never been so proud of being part of something. Thank you for that moment, and for the picture. My sisters will be pleased with this and JT's picture."

"Oh?"

"They complain that my apartment is a bit under decorated. These will make it practically homey."

She laughed. "Is it really that bad?"

"Well, I'd say it was functional. That is not how they put it, however. Your house is definitely a home." He hurried out to his coat and came back with a small box. "I got you something, too. Well, you and Jamie."

She opened it and found a book. *Memories.*

"It's like a diary. I thought you could write Jamie notes. Notes about his father. Maybe even ask the chief and Mrs. Martin to add some. That way, Jamie will have something more than pictures of his father. I got a second one. I thought I'd take it to the station and ask the guys who worked with Jay to do the same thing. I know it's not—"

Laura interrupted him, ran over and hugged him. "That was the most considerate gift I ever..." Her tears were coming too rapidly for her to finish the sentence.

"Hey, I should give credit where credit is due. My mom did something along those lines for us."

"Yes, but this wasn't your mom. It was all you. Thank you, Seth. And I hope that you'll consider putting in some entries."

"Sure." He looked his watch. "I've got to go. I'm working tonight to help out. I always feel bad for guys with families during the holidays. Sorry. You said you wanted to be alone."

She shook her head. "I thought I did, but now I'm glad I wasn't. You, the Martins and JT all came over and helped make today...special. Thank you for that."

He kissed her forehead platonically. "Anytime."

She followed him to the door. "Merry Christmas, Seth."

"Merry Christmas, Laura." He looked up and pointed.

Laura looked up, too, and saw a sprig of mistletoe. "How did you get that there?"

"Not me. Maybe Santa." He leaned down and kissed her. It was platonic...almost. Maybe his lips lingered a fraction too long.

Maybe hers softened a little too much under the pressure of his.

"Should we talk about it?" he asked.

"Not today," she said.

He nodded. "I should let you go."

"Seth?" He stopped. Laura stood on tiptoe and kissed him again. "I'm not ready to talk, and I'm not sure exactly what this is, but I like doing that."

"Me, too." He leaned down and kissed her again. "Merry Christmas, Laura."

"Merry Christmas, Seth."

AT THE STATION, COMPLETING a report, Seth felt a semblance of normalcy. Lately, work was the only place where he felt this way.

He hadn't intended on kissing Laura again. He understood it was too soon for her. Hell, there was a very good chance it was too soon for him.

Two damaged people coming together...

There was every possibility that it wouldn't end well, and one or both of them might get hurt.

Laura had said he was a hero. A hero would pull back and give her room.

He'd tried that before and hadn't managed it. He couldn't seem to stay away.

When he was with Laura he felt happy, content. He felt alive.

And he thought when she was with him, she felt the same.

Maybe they could help each other.

Maybe. It was a word that spoke of hope.

It had been a long time since Seth was hopeful, but he was that and so many other things now...thanks to Laura.

THAT NIGHT, AFTER JAMIE went to bed, Laura got ready for bed. She took off her rings as she lotioned her hands. And for the first time, she didn't put her engagement ring back on. She put it, and the ring the Martins had given her, in a small bowl on her dresser. She'd save them for Jamie.

"Goodbye, Jay," she whispered out loud.

She stared at them for a while and then thought about kissing Seth.

She hadn't been ready before, and she wasn't sure she was ready for it now, but she definitely thought she might be someday.

Laura found the leather-bound notebook Seth had given her and stared at the rich pages for a moment, then wrote:

Dear Jamie,
Today is your first Christmas, and despite everything, you're very lucky. You have me, who loves you beyond everything else. There will never come a day when that love fades. And you have two men who loved you as well. Your father. I know he would have given anything to stay here, to know you. And it may be a silly idea, but I believe that he sent Seth to watch over you since he can't. Seth bought this notebook as a Christmas gift for you, so that I can write down stories of your father. It was a sweet gift. You should know your father.
So, here we go.
I met Jay...

CHAPTER ELEVEN

THERE WAS A QUIET, NEW rhythm to Seth's life that revolved around work and Laura.

In the weeks following Christmas, he spent most of his nonworking waking hours at her house. They didn't talk about their growing physical attraction, but they continued flirting with it. Long, hot kisses good-night. And casual touches that were anything but.

They both knew they were playing with fire.

It was easier when JT was there. She served as a buffer. Seth would entertain Jamie which meant JT and Laura had uninterrupted time together. He loved watching the two of them. Laura helped JT with her reading. She was patient, even when JT became frustrated.

He was amazed by the progress the girl was making. But with him and Laura there was no progress. There was no regression. There was no talking about what was happening between them. They were standing in the midst of a quagmire—in danger of losing their footing at any moment. When he wasn't with her, he worried that they were going to make some false step. And when he was with her, all he could think about was her.

Today, JT barreled in and threw her book bag on the table with a loud thud.

"JT?" Laura asked.

"Something wrong?" He juggled Jamie on his shoulder, waiting for a burp.

"You remember that English test on *Pride and Prejudice*?" JT slumped into one of the chairs.

"Yes," Laura said slowly.

"Well, I read that book with you, and even watched that long PBS miniseries, and the new movie, too. I was ready for the test. Knew all the vocab. I should have done good on it."

"Oh, JT..." Laura started as Seth said, "Hey, it's okay."

"No, it's not okay, because I didn't do good, I rocked it." She pulled the test from her backpack, jumped from the chair and held it up. "I mean, the brainiacs in our class might think a B- isn't that impressive, but, Ms. Watson, I don't think I ever got a B anything in an English class, ever. Not even once."

She tossed the test on the table and hugged Laura, then turned and hugged Seth, too, squeezing Jamie in between them.

JT picked up the test and handed it to Laura. "I think Ms. Lutz must have shit a brick when she had to give me something higher than a D."

Laura studied it. "JT, that's not fair. No teacher likes seeing students struggle."

"No good teacher like you. But Mrs. Lutz is old and tired. She hates teaching now. And she really hates teaching me."

"JT..." Laura obviously didn't know what to say.

Seth supplied, "Well, the grade isn't about Mrs. Lutz, or even Ms. Watson. It's about you and how hard you've been working." Jamie finally burped, as if for emphasis.

"Yeah, but it's about you guys, too. You are the first grown-ups who ever really cared. And I know I'm a kid, but I'm old enough to know that's special." She beamed at them, clearly grateful.

"So we should celebrate, if you want? Dinner? You'd have to call your mom and see if it's okay. Maybe she'd like to join us?" Seth offered. They'd invited JT's mom to other events, but she'd never accepted. She never even got out of the car when she picked JT up.

JT said she was pleased to have someone else looking after her, because it gave her mom more time with the new boyfriend.

"That'd be great. Let me call her. I don't think she'll come, but I'll ask." JT whipped her cell phone from her pocket and dialed, then walked into the living room.

"That's nice of you, Seth." Laura held out the test so he could see it as well.

"I should have asked if you minded taking Jamie out." He took the test and studied it. "She did great. I think that after watching Colin Firth in the miniseries, I could probably have taken the test, too. And you don't know how unmanly that admission makes me feel."

Laura laughed and kissed his cheek. "You, sir, are the epitome of manliness. I'm so proud of JT I could burst with it. As for checking, I don't mind taking Jamie out, but I could..." She hesitated, then quickly said, "I could call the Martins and see if they'd like to watch Jamie for a couple hours."

Seth raised a brow.

Laura took a deep breath and nodded. "Mrs. Martin nearly swooned with happiness when she watched him while I got my hair cut."

"Are things still strained between you?"

"Yes, but they do love Jamie, and for his sake I try to make sure they see him a couple times a week."

"How about you seeing them?" he asked.

"Of course, I see them. They come here. Or I see them when I drop him off in order to run an errand."

"Laura, that's not what I meant. They're your family."

She shook her head. "They were Jay's family and only tolerated me for his sake."

"I don't think that's true, and I suspect, neither do you."

"Seth, I don't want to fight, but seriously, of all the people who could give me family-relationship advice, you're not high on my list of counselors given your relationship with your parents. You've never explained why and—"

JT returned but seemed oblivious to the tension that twanged between Seth and Laura.

Seth should have known better than to bring up the Martins. He avoided mentioning them, she avoided mentioning his family. It worked that way.

JT looked upset. "Mom said she had other plans for dinner, not that that's a surprise. But she doesn't care if I go with you guys."

Seth saw Laura's look of concern. "Well, good. We've got some serious celebrating to do. How about Laura calls the chief to see if we're taking Jamie or they are, and then we hit the road."

"I'll go call now," Laura said.

"Well done, My Lady." Seth gave a deep, formal bow to JT, while he juggled the baby.

JT giggled exactly like a teenage girl. "Well, Sir Seth, may I take Sir Jamie for a bit? Yesterday he was showing me his new trick."

"New trick? What is this new trick I know nothing about?" He handed the baby over to her.

"Watch." JT sat on the floor next to the baby play mat Jamie had got for Christmas.

She positioned him directly underneath the stuffed zebra. Jamie reached for it, and batted at it with his hand.

"He likes the zebra the best, but he's reaching for all the toys now, trying to grab them."

"Wow, should he be able to do that already?" Seth asked.

"I don't know," JT said. "But he's a smart boy."

"Smart? I'm going to go with he's a prodigy." Seth leaned down to the baby. "Look at you, big man."

"Sir Big Man, remember," JT teased.

"Sir Big Man." Seth held the baby up so they were eye-to-eye. "Sir Big Man's quite the prodigy."

The baby giggled.

"Hey, he likes it," Seth said.

JT took him and said, "Sir Big Man," much to Jamie's giggly delight.

"Yep, he's a Sir Big Man, toy-grabbing prodigy."

For the rest of the evening, Laura felt out of sorts, ever since she stood in the doorway and watched Seth and JT play with Jamie. Seth was joking and kidding around with both kids, and her heart had melted.

She felt whole. How could she feel so happy and content when Jay was dead?

She put it in the most brutal terms. No easy euphemisms. He hadn't passed. He wasn't gone. He hadn't moved on to a better place. He was dead, as hard and finite as that.

Jay—the man she loved—was gone, and not only was she happy, she was attracted to another man. She and Seth had avoided any talk of that attraction, but it was there. It was palpable whenever she was with him.

And it was growing.

Laura was more confused than she'd been in her whole life. Every emotion toyed with the next until she didn't know what she felt. The only respite she had was when Seth held her or kissed her. The most casual touch was enough.

But those moments always ended, and she was thrown back into the tumult.

She thought she had successfully hidden her feelings during dinner, and when they picked up the baby at the Martins, but Seth kept shooting her looks that told her she wasn't managing as well as she hoped.

"HEY, PENNY FOR YOUR THOUGHTS?" Seth asked Laura, at her house later that evening. Laura had seemed distracted all night, and he wasn't sure why. He knew she was happy on JT's behalf, but somehow she didn't seem quite happy enough. Something was bothering her.

"I'm not sure about whether to go back to school right after Valentine's Day, or wait until the fall. I'm torn."

He came over to the couch, sat next to her and put his arm around her. "He'll be fine no matter what you decide. He's loved. Babies sense that."

"I know he will, but I'm not sure I will. I like surety. I like knowing where I stand. I don't like feeling undecided. One day I'm sure I want to go back in a month, and the next day Jamie does something amazing and I know waiting until next school year is the best decision."

Seth leaned down and kissed her forehead. "It will all be okay."

He wished he had some answer for her. Some wise words to make everything better, but he didn't.

"How can being torn in two be okay?" Laura asked.

Suddenly, Seth wondered if they were talking about more than Laura going back to school. "Laura, I—"

She shook her head. "Talk to me about work. About anything. Something to distract me."

He reached out and brushed a strand of her blond hair behind her ear. It was silky. He loved the way it felt, which distracted him from distracting her. He searched for something. "Remember those kids I took home a while back? The exchange student and graffiti kids?"

She nodded and that strand of blond hair slid back across her cheek. "How could I forget? JT was already in trouble for skipping school and lying to you. She's come a long way since."

He resisted the urge to retuck it. "I checked in on Joel, the kid who was in love."

"His mom was at her wit's end, right?"

"Right. Anyway, I got him involved with the Police Cadets at the station, and his mom is thrilled with the change in him. She got him a Skype account and he talks to Lisa after school most nights."

"So, you're a matchmaker? You kept Romeo and Juliet from being totally pulled apart."

"Technology did that. I have kept an eye on him, and his mom says things have been much better at home. That's one of my favorite parts of the job—when I feel I've made a difference."

"You're a Keller, through and through, Seth." She nodded, as if agreeing with herself, and her hair bob-bled about, brushing against her cheek.

Seth couldn't resist the temptation and pushed it back behind her ear again. "What do you mean?"

"The entire Keller family seems to go out of their way to help other people. It started with your parents adopting six kids—kids who've carried on their legacy. You're a cop. Dom's a physical therapist. Your sister's a nurse. Zac runs the grocery store, but he's found a way to turn that into a community asset by hiring kids in trouble, or special people. Your whole family has turned giving into an art form. That's a rare gift. I should know, since I've only recently been Kellerized."

His hand stilled, resting on her shoulder. "Kellerized?"

"Eli used that phrase when she was here with Tucker. I like it. I don't think I've thanked you enough for taking me and Jamie under your wing. I..." Laura let the sentence trail off and simply leaned toward him and kissed him, full on the lips. No hesitation. No holding back.

Seth wanted her. He'd wanted her for a long time, but he wasn't sure this was the time. Since that first kiss when they'd clarified their relationship as friends, they'd toyed with it being something more. But despite their joking about no huge exterior obstacles, there was something worse than pairing a cop with an international art thief, or a vegan and carnivore.

There was baggage. They both had things in the past that held them back from the future.

He knew it was time to let go of Allie, to move on. But he hadn't quite managed it yet, and he knew Laura was still mourning Jay. Getting any more involved with each other could lead to pain for both of them.

He tried to hold on to those thoughts—on to the reasons why he and Laura shouldn't let this go any further than they already had, but she toyed with the buttons on his shirt and he forgot those very sensible reasons why they shouldn't do what he suspected they might do.

He stilled her hand by placing his over it and broke off the kiss. "Laura, I don't think you want to do this."

"No, what I don't want is to think. To weigh or analyze this. I don't want to feel guilty about being alive, about being happy. All I do know is that I want you. I've wanted you for a while now." She paused and added, "Unless you don't want me."

"No, I guarantee that's not the issue." Wanting Laura. That feeling had grown exponentially. Every moment he spent with her. Every touch. Every kiss. The wanting kept growing until he hardly knew how to contain it.

But she deserved more than just his desire, and he wasn't sure he could give her that. He liked her. Loved her as a friend even. But more?

He wasn't sure. "Laura, we need to stop and think this through. I don't want you to wake up tomorrow and regret this."

"I won't," she said with a surety he doubted.

"But..."

She stood, took his hand and pulled him to his feet. "Jamie's down until one or so. We have time and I want you. This doesn't have to be more than that. Simply two friends wanting each other. Friends with benefits."

"Laura."

"If you don't want—" she started.

Seth couldn't lie. "I do want. I want a lot. But I don't know if that's enough."

"For tonight, it is." She sounded so sure. She led him to her room and he followed.

For tonight, desire might be enough for both of them, but Seth worried that tomorrow it might not be.

But the worry faded as he made love to Laura.

In every fiber of his being it felt right.

She felt right.

And he hoped that would be enough...for both of them.

LAURA STARED AT THE MAN sleeping next to her. What had she done? Well, to begin with, she'd irrevocably altered their relation ship.

Making love to Seth had felt right, but now that the moment was over, Laura felt awkward. And naked. Naked in a way that had very little to do with not having on any clothes.

"Are you okay?" Seth asked from the other side of the bed.

Rather than snuggling after, they'd each moved to their own side of the bed. Laura nodded in the dimly lit room. "Yeah. I'm fine. You?"

She felt, rather than saw him nod as well. "Yeah."

Seth was her best friend. That should have made the aftermath of making love easier, but instead, it seemed to make it harder. "I don't know what to do now," she confessed.

"What do you mean?" he asked.

"I mean, I've never had casual sex, and don't know what to do...after. Do we both go to sleep and you stay over? It wouldn't be the first time I'd made us coffee in the morning. Or do you get up, pick up your clothes and leave. How do people do casual?"

"I think we can handle this in whatever manner feels right to us, but don't kid yourself, Laura. This wasn't casual, it's not... What did you call it? Friends with benefits? It's not that, either, and I think we both know that. We've been heading here for a long time."

She remained silent.

"But neither one of us is ready. So what do we do?" he asked.

"Seth, remember when we were joking about not having some huge conflict standing between us? No cop and art thief here. Nothing big and tangible. If that's what we try to tell ourselves, I think we're both lying to ourselves. We may not have Romeo and Juliet feuding families, but we do have things to overcome."

"Maybe it's time we dealt with some of those things. We've skirted around them and know the basics. Maybe it's time for more than that. Tell me about you and Jay. About you and his parents." Seth pulled her into his arms.

Laura relaxed against his chest, not looking at him helped as she forced the story. "It happened so fast. One moment, Jay was getting ready for work. It was a normal evening. We talked about the baby, about the wedding. He left and I went to bed. The next thing I knew, it was morning and everything I thought I knew, all my plans and dreams died with him. The doctor said that was it. Jay wasn't coming back." Her voice broke and she forced herself not to cry.

"I was at his bedside with his parents in the hospital talking about how to handle his death. Jay had made his wishes clear. He asked me to be sure he didn't end his life tethered to a machine.

He asked me, Seth. He trusted me and I couldn't do it for him. I don't know how to get past that."

"And you blame the chief and Mrs. Martin?" Seth asked gently.

That gentleness just about did her in. She could feel the tears welling in her eyes, but as she thought about that moment in the hospital, about Mrs. Martin's words, her anger flashed white-hot and burned her tears away.

"Of course, I blame them. Jay asked me to do that for him and they wouldn't listen. His mother wouldn't let go." All that anger she thought she'd beaten just rose again.

"But you haven't let go, either," Seth pointed out. "I don't think you're really mad at Jay's parents. Don't you think he'd have agreed to hang in there for a week if it would have helped his mother?"

"Yeah. If I'm not mad at them, who am I mad at?" She sat up and pulled the sheet to herself, feeling every bit exposed.

"You're angry at Jay. For leaving you."

"Oh, really, how can I be mad at Jay? He didn't choose to get sick. He didn't choose to die—to leave me and Jamie. I know that."

"Knowing and feeling—those are two different things. And I know it because I've been thinking about my parents—more specifically, my relationship with them—a lot lately. I was mad when I was younger and they wanted me to wait to marry Allie. I vowed that we'd make it on our own, and we did. When she died..."

Laura's anger ebbed because she knew this was as hard on him as it was on her. "Tell me," she said. "I know Allie died, I know about the twins, but that's it. How did she die?"

"She was six months pregnant. And huge. So giant. But rather than resent the changes in her body, she reveled in them. She called me, the day she died, crying hysterically that she was losing the babies. I told her to hang up and I called 911, then the doctor. I raced home in my cruiser. Lights and sirens. I got there right after the first responders. They'd kicked in the front door when she didn't answer."

His voice cracked as he spoke. She reached across the bed and took his hand.

"There's a term, placental abruption. I'd never heard of it till that day, but I'll never forget it." His voice broke as he said the term. "Her placenta was lower than it should have been and it ruptured. They found her on the kitchen floor. I rushed my wife to the hospital and..." He stopped and was silent.

Laura squeezed his hand, and finally, he squeezed back. His words came out soft and hoarse. "There was nothing that anyone could have done. I was angry. As angry as you are. But how could I be mad at her? It's not like she planned it, any more than Jay could have. My parents were great targets for all that anger. I mean, there they were, crying and saying they'd loved Allie. They'd had a fit when we married right out of high school, and now they were crying? They were being hypocrites, and I was pissed..."

Laura spoke then, as gently as he had. "Because being mad at them was easier than being mad at Allie."

"Yes. And after a while, it was second nature. I just avoided them. But since you came into my life, I've been with my family more than I've been in years. It's as if having you and Jamie around makes me remember how great my parents are. I've called my mother intending to talk it out. But when I get her on the phone, I realize I've forgotten how to talk to her. I know she loves me. She loves me enough to let me be mad at her because without that anger, I don't know if I could have made it. But I'm not angry anymore. And I miss my parents."

"I'm glad. You should talk to them."

"And you should talk to the Martins."

She shook her head. "It's different. Your parents are yours—they love you. The Martins are Jay's parents. They loved him and tolerated me."

"That's not right, Laura."

"We're really doing this? Lying naked in bed after making love and talking about Allie, Jay, your parents and the Martins?"

"Laura."

Softly, she admitted, "I look at Jamie and know I'd do anything for him. Even hang on to him when he was past the point of no return."

"I know he's somebody else's baby, but I feel the same way. I'd do anything for him. I'd hold out hope long after it was gone. I'd do everything I could to keep him from marrying too soon. I want to see him go to college, get a job, fall in love, have children..."

"So where does that leave us?" Laura asked.

"Maybe we both need to take a break from whatever *this* is and put our pasts to rest before we see where our future lies."

"I don't know if I'm ready to put my past to rest. I want to, but I'm not sure I can," she said.

"And I don't know if we can go any further than this until we do," he said simply. "We could have something special, Laura, and I don't want to screw it up by rushing things."

"You want me to go to Jay's parents and what? Forgive them for not giving him the ending he wanted? For preventing him from dying with dignity? You didn't see it. There was a tube down his throat. Machines beeping. An IV. The scene haunts me. And I should just put it aside? I see the Martins. I let them see Jamie. But you want more than that?"

"I want you to talk to them. Maybe you'll forgive them. Maybe you'll find there's nothing to forgive. We need to cool this..." he said as he waved a hand between them, "...whatever this is, and sort out our feelings, our families."

"What if we can't?"

Seth didn't answer.

Laura didn't blame him. She didn't know what to say, either.

Seth dressed and let himself out of the house. She stood in the dark foyer, a quilt around her shoulders.

She walked to the window. Seth's truck was parked under the streetlight in front of the house. He was clearly illuminated as he opened the door.

Before crawling in, he looked up at her window, as if he could see her in the dark house, and waved.

She waved back and couldn't help but wonder if this was an ending...or a new beginning.

Without him she felt empty. Her mind jumped from thought to thought so quickly she couldn't hold on to, much less process, any of them.

It seemed her life had been in flux so long that she couldn't remember a time when it wasn't.

Back in her bedroom, she didn't need anything more than the glow from the streetlight coming through her window to find the dish that held her rings.

She picked them both up and held them. She wanted to cry. Cry about Jay. About the Martins. And yes, cry about Seth. But she'd already cried oceans of tears. She held them back now, feeling them build, like too much water behind a dam.

But she knew if she started crying, she might not be able to stop.

She let the rings fall back into the dish with tiny clinks.

As if on cue, Jamie's whimpering could be heard over the baby monitor. She headed to his room. Laura was thankful. Caring for Jamie gave her something to think about other than all the things she needed to think about.

She looked down at her son as she nursed him, and stroked the peach-fuzz on top of his head.

Jamie smiled at her, a thin trail of milk dribbling down his cheek.

The tears she held at bay eased.

Laura knew she had a lot to come to terms with, but right now, she knew one thing with utter certainty. She'd do anything for her son. She loved him more than she'd ever imagined.

Later, with Jamie asleep and the memory book on her lap, she wrote:

Dear Jamie,
Tonight's entry isn't about your father.

Writing those stories about Jay for her son had let her say goodbye to Jay in a way she'd never expected. But tonight was something else.

As I nursed you tonight, I realized that I love you. Oh, I knew that before. From the moment that you were born, I was hit with such a wave of love, I don't know how to describe it. You'll understand it when you have a child of your own and hold him or her for the first time.

It's just tonight, everything felt out of control and I had no idea what to do about anything...then you woke up for your feeding and as I held you, that love I felt simply overpowered all my worries and doubts.

I love you.

And I know that no matter what happens, I have you. I have you and I love you.

I wanted to put that down so that someday, if you're feeling lost and confused, maybe you'll read this and it will help you as much as it helped me.

No matter how crazy my life is, I have you to center me. Thank you for that.

I will always be here for you.

Love,
 Mom

CHAPTER TWELVE

BEFORE GETTING OUT OF BED, Seth lay there a long time, trying to figure out what the hell he'd done the night before. He'd been with a woman he cared about. Then, rather than enjoying the moment and hoping for other moments to follow, he'd put a halt to it.

When Joel had cried that he wasn't ready to say goodbye to Lisa, the exchange student, Seth had empathized. He hadn't been ready to say goodbye to Allie, either. But last night, he'd walked away from Laura.

He hadn't said goodbye, but he'd put distance between them. He'd talked about their problems and healing, but in the light of day, he wasn't sure if that made him a good guy who was trying to save them both from pain, or a coward, running away from Laura and trying to say it was for her sake. He wanted to think of himself as a good guy, but he suspected he might be a schmuck.

He stood in his small kitchen, staring into the living area. His apartment seemed more barren than ever, despite JT's drawing and the picture of him holding Jamie.

Looking at the picture made him think of all the photos that lined his mother's walls. All the kids on their Homecomings. If you looked closely, beneath the smiles there was an undercurrent of fear in every one. Each wondering if this really was home, or just another in a long line of temporary stops.

Group photos. Some posed, some candid. There was one of him, May and his mom that he loved. They'd made a tent in the middle of the living room and his mom had come in to tell them it was time to tidy up, but rather than do that, she'd joined them in the tent. When their dad got home, he'd snapped the photo of all three of them laughing as they peeked out of the tent's opening.

Seth wanted Laura to work things out with the Martins, but their pain was fresh and new. He'd let the damaged relationship go on with his parents for years, first because of misplaced anger, then because of awkwardness. It was time for him to pony up and fix things. Partly because he wanted things to work out between himself and Laura and he truly didn't believe they could unless he dumped what he'd been carrying around for so long. But mainly he knew it was time. He missed his parents deeply.

He swallowed his coffee in a gulp and half an hour later was on his way to Whedon. Within minutes of passing the I-90 ridge, there was easily an extra foot of snow covering the landscape, though the road itself was clear. The road crews in this area of the country were accustomed to snow...and lots of it. Despite today's accumulation, the drive to Whedon seemed faster than it normally did.

He pulled up in front of his parents' house and sat in the truck, staring at the front porch. It was bare now. His dad had taken the Christmas lights and decorations down. Mom liked to unholiday the house right after the New Year.

They'd all been so happy growing up here.

Their friends had gravitated to the house. It wasn't that his mom always had something in the oven or cooling on the counter. It was a feeling of welcome. His mom and dad had welcomed each of their children into their home and hearts. They'd welcomed their children's friends as wholeheartedly, too.

They'd welcomed Allie when he started dating her. But after he announced they were getting married right after graduation, that feeling of welcome had evaporated.

He stared at the house and tried to remember everything that had happened, but it was so long ago. He remembered his parents had asked him to wait to marry Allie until after college. He remembered the look of disappointment on his mother's face. Disapproval on his father's.

He'd shouted that if they didn't approve, that was fine. He was an adult and didn't need their permission. He'd married Allie at the courthouse in Erie. Just the two of them. Their

242

witnesses had been two random clerks the judge had asked.

Because they were married they didn't need their parents' income details on the college financial aid forms and qualified for a lot of help. And they'd both worked. His memories of those years centered around being tired. Exhausted.

It had been hard, but he and Allie had done it. Their marriage occasionally stumbled, but it survived.

His parents had been wrong about that, but they'd been right about how hard it had been. If he and Allie had waited, it might have been easier. They could have dated through college. Gone out. Hung out. They could have stayed kids, rather than jump feet first into adulthood.

They'd made it harder on themselves. But in the end, he'd had so few years with Allie, even those exhausting college years together were something he'd never trade away.

He thought of Jamie. What if Jamie was a teen and said he wanted to marry? Seth was sure that Laura would balk, and he knew he'd fight against it because he wouldn't want Jamie to go through what he'd gone through. Now he could understand his parents' position better than he ever had. And if he were honest, he'd admit that even though his parents hadn't approved, they'd never cut him or Allie off.

He'd done that.

And after Allie died, heaping more anger on them didn't take much effort.

He'd rehashed this over and over in his head. Now it was time to tell his parents. To apologize and try to understand their point of view.

He'd meant what he said to Laura. He didn't think they could move on unless they both put their pasts to rest.

Doing that started here for him.

What if it was too late?

Though his parents had shown time and again that they missed him, and forgave him, he still felt nervous.

He'd been three when he'd come home. He didn't remember it. Or his birth mother, or the foster homes he'd stayed in when she was jailed. He didn't remember her taking him back, then losing custody. He'd been too young for actual memories, but maybe a part of him, on some emotional level, hadn't forgotten.

This morning felt as important as that first Homecoming. And maybe, on some level, he felt the same fear of rejection.

It had been years since he'd simply shown up to talk to his parents. He walked up to the door and paused. He would have knocked last week. It was a way to emphasize that he no longer felt like part of the family. But it was more than that, it was a way to hurt his mother and father.

Today, he simply opened the door and let himself in. The house smelled of fresh bread. His mom hated store-bought bread. She used to make two or three loaves a day when they were younger. He felt badly that he didn't know how often she made bread now.

"Mom?" he called.

"In the kitchen," came her response.

He should have known.

Most of his memories of seeing his mom were in the kitchen. He'd snatch a warm-from-the-oven cookie as he discussed his day at school. Or he'd help with dishes when the chore fell to him—only it wasn't really a chore when his mom was there. She'd pass him a warm, wet dish and as he dried it, they'd talk about anything and everything.

His mom turned around as he entered the kitchen. "Seth? Is something wrong?" There was a sense of panic in her voice.

"No, Mom. Nothing's wrong." She visibly relaxed at his words. "I want to speak to you and Dad."

She took another loaf of bread from the oven and placed it on a rack to cool. "Your dad's at the store filling in for Zac. He took Eli and the kids to spend the weekend at the hotel on Peach Street. The one with Splash Lagoon, that indoor water park."

Seth nodded. "Yes, I know the one."

"They're still bonding with Ebony. She's adjusting well, but before she came to them, there were issues. They thought a weekend with only the four of them was a good idea. I do, too. I was thinking about that Cook Forest weekend."

He smiled. "You rented that cabin and Dad took us canoeing down the river. He said he was an Eagle Scout, so of course he knew how to canoe." He smiled. "He dumped us all into the water."

"He never said he earned an Eagle Scout canoeing badge." His mom smiled.

He'd missed this—talking to his mom, sharing family stories and jokes. "Mom, I need to say..."

Her expression quickly changed from smiling to serious.

"Are you okay?" he asked.

She didn't answer the question. Instead, she said, "I'll confess, I'm a bit scared. You don't wander into the kitchen to talk to me anymore." Her voice sounded low and husky, as if she might cry. She picked up a knife and sliced into one of the brown loaves cooling on the counter. She put a piece on a plate and slid it in front of him. No butter. No topping. That's how he'd always eaten his oven-warm bread.

He looked at the bread and knew it was more than just food. His mother showed her love in so many tangible ways, and food had always been a big part of that.

He'd planned to start with, *I'm sorry*, but what came out was, "I think I'm falling for Laura."

His mother approached, as if she were going to pat his hand, then stopped. "Honey, that's not news to anyone who's seen you two together."

"But we're taking a break."

"Why?"

"Because it's too soon for her. And we both have a lot to deal with first. My coming here, it's part of my baggage." The words that needed to be said weighed heavily on his tongue, just like they did when he'd arrived here as a kid and hadn't spoken. But he was no longer an intimidated child. This time, he had to talk. "After Allie, I was so angry. I was pissed at the world, and I was pissed at you and Dad. I told you it was because you were hypocrites, that you hadn't approved of our marriage, yet mourned her death, but that wasn't really it. It's hard to be mad at the whole world—especially when I'm out there, working with people every day—so I narrowed my focus, and you and Dad were easy targets."

"I understood, Seth. You needed someone to be mad at and you trusted us enough to be mad at us. You suffered a loss not for the first time. When you came home to us, you'd lost foster parents, then your birth mother. You were so little and hurt. You were terrified."

"Yes, but though that boy was terrified, there you were and you told me that you loved me, that I was special and that I could do anything. You taught me to try to make a difference. And I believed you and I tried. I became a cop to do just that." He pulled an inside piece of bread up and rolled it into a ball like he used to when he was young, but he didn't eat it. He picked another small piece and rolled it, too.

"Even when I was mad at you because you and Dad didn't support my marriage to Allie, I knew you loved me. I was young and cocky, but at heart, I knew you only worried because you loved me. And I still believed you. I still believed I could do anything. And then we found out about the babies, and my life...I'd never been so happy. And then..."

"Then Allie died," his mother whispered.

He crushed the small piece of bread in his hand. "She was dead, and I realized you had lied to me. I couldn't do anything. I couldn't save her. I couldn't save our children."

"Seth." This time she did take his hand. "I know you'd have done anything to save Allie. She knew that, too."

His voice dropped. "It got worse. Because what if I lost Allie and the babies, and I still went on and lived a life that had some meaning? What kind of love can go on after that kind of loss?"

"Seth..." Pain filled his mother's voice. She gently squeezed his hand. "I've always loved you, Seth. And even when I've made mistakes it was love that drove me. It was the same for you."

"Somewhere, deep inside I knew that you would always love me, no matter what."

"We always loved Allie. We just thought you weren't ready and we worried—"

Tiny bread balls littered his plate. "I get that now. But I needed someone to be mad at, and there you were."

"What's changed now?"

"Me. I've changed because of Laura and the baby. I understand why you objected to Allie and me marrying so young. I'd have done that and so much more for my kids. Even though I know I hurt you, you waited. You took it. You trusted that I'd find my way back. Well, I finally did. And I'm so sorry."

"Seth, I'd have waited as long as I needed to to hear those words and have you come home to me...again." She gripped his hand tightly, as if she were afraid that he'd slip away if she let go. "So what are you going to do about Laura?"

"I'm going to be her friend until she figures out we can be so much more than that."

"And if she doesn't?" his mother asked.

"I learned from an expert that if you give someone the time they need, they'll find their way home. I'm Laura's home and I trust she'll find her way to me in her own time."

Losing Allie hurt. It always would. But loving Laura didn't diminish what he'd felt for Allie. His heart was big enough to love them both. There was no competition. Just as there was no competition between him and Jay.

Love wasn't about winning or losing.

"I have a very wise son."

"No, you have a son who's a dolt. But I'm lucky enough to have a family who loves me anyway—a family who taught me how to be persistent. So, I wait."

"We'll wait with you."

Seth hugged his mom. Hugged her in a way he hadn't in years.

"So, what is this?" his dad asked as he took a large sniff of fresh-baked bread.

Seth knew he had to explain it all to his dad, too, but that could wait. He walked over and hugged his father, who, without hesitation, returned the hug. "I'm sorry, Dad. Sorry for everything."

"We're family, Seth. There's nothing to be sorry for."

But there was, and Seth knew it.

His mom came over and joined in the hugging. And there, enveloped in his parents' arms, he felt as if he'd finally let go of his past and come home. It was the start of a second homecoming for him. But that was all it was. He wouldn't truly be home again without Laura and Jamie.

He loved them both.

He loved Laura.

There it was. He loved her and he'd finally healed enough to admit it.

Seth could only hope Laura would heal, too.

He looked at his parents, who'd waited for him without complaint and knew he'd find the strength to wait for her. How could he not, with such good examples?

THERE WAS SOMETHING DIFFERENT about Seth.

Laura could see it in his face on Sunday when he came to the door. She opened it and found him setting the shovel against the house.

He glanced up at her and grinned. "It's snowing like crazy."

She could have scolded, could have insisted that she knew how to shovel, but she knew Seth wouldn't listen any more than the guys in Jay's group. She hadn't shoveled once this season. "Thanks."

Seth had called, although he hadn't stopped by since they'd made love. Not that she'd been sitting alone in the house. Two of her colleagues from school had visited. JT had come by to work on a research paper for English. The Martins stopped in to see Jamie. But, despite all the commotion, the house had seemed quiet without Seth. She realized he was still standing on the porch. "Come on in."

He did as if nothing had happened. As if nothing had changed. He hung his coat on the same hook he always did. He leaned down and kissed her cheek. His lips felt cold against her skin, and it had nothing to do with the cold temperature outside.

"Can I get you something to drink?" she asked, feeling unsure. A few nights ago he'd made love to her, then told her they needed to cool down their relationship until she'd healed. Now he was here...

"No, but thanks. This is a quick visit. I'm on my way to the station. I said I'd do a few hours overtime before my actual shift starts."

She led him into the living room and she sat on the couch. She noticed he sat in the chair across from her.

"Laura?"

"I have something to ask you," she blurted out before she could talk herself out of it.

"Sure."

"I talked to our minister this morning after church. I'm planning Jamie's baptism and wondered if you'd consider being his godfather? I mean, I know you want to..." She searched for the right description. "Cool things off between us, but I also know you care about Jamie. And I can't think of anyone I'd rather have as his godfather than you."

He didn't hesitate at all, but answered immediately, "I'd be honored."

"Thank you." It felt so formal between them. Laura missed their easy intimacy. "I think it's going to be on St. Patrick's Day. Jay's favorite day of the year was St. Patrick's Day. He's still got a couple great-aunts over in Ireland."

"What about his parents?"

"No, they don't live in Ireland," she teased, hoping to avoid talking about the Martins.

Seth gave her a look that said he saw through her attempt at humor.

"I'm sure they'll be at the baptism," she tried.

"That's not what I meant and you know it."

"We're getting along fine. They were here yesterday to see Jamie."

"Have you talked to them? Really talked?"

"Have you talked to your parents? Really talked?" she countered.

"Yes," he said, quietly. "It was hard, but I apologized. My mom... I hurt her so much. It was easier to be angry at my parents than face where my anger was really coming from. I was mad at myself. I was so mad, Laura, and there was nowhere to funnel that anger, so my parents were perfect targets."

"We had this conversation. We seem to keep circling around to the fact that you think I'm upset at Jay for dying, for leaving me alone with our son, and since I can't be mad at a dead man—" she flinched at the words "—I've decided to be mad at his parents, but I don't buy that. I didn't decide to be mad at them. You didn't hear the way his mother spoke to me at the hospital."

"I don't think you decided to be mad at them—the head has nothing to do with feelings, does it?"

"I'm drawing up a will and naming the Martins as Jamie's legal guardians in case anything happens to me. How mad can I be if I'm entrusting them with my son?"

"Laura, I don't want to fight about this. I just dropped in to check on you and Jamie. I thought I should stay away, but as you can see, I only managed a couple days. I miss you—it's as simple and complex as that. And I'm honored to be Jamie's godfather."

"You miss me, but you're still going to give me some distance until you've declared me healed."

"No."

"Yes," she argued. "You took years after Allie died, and I've had months. And just like that, because Seth Keller's declared it so, I'm supposed to say, 'Yes, my baggage is gone.'"

"Laura, you're not being fair. I don't want to hurry you into something you can't handle yet."

"No, you want whatever this is between us to be on your terms."

"Not my terms. I simply love you enough to wait. You're right, you need more time. I'm going to be your friend and give you all the time you need."

"You what?"

Rather than repeating himself, he said, "Listen, I'd better be going." Seth leaned down and gave her the most platonic of kisses on her forehead. Laura knew that he thought he was being noble, pulling away from her, but it didn't feel noble to her. It felt cowardly.

Well, she wasn't about to sit back and have Seth proclaim when she was up for more than friendship. So she took his police uniform's collar in her hands, ignoring the bite of his lapel pins, and pulled his face to hers. Then she kissed him. Kissed him with all her pent-up feelings.

Kissed him as if she might never stop kissing him.

She wasn't sure how long she'd have continued, but Jamie's cry sounded loud and clear, and brought her back to the present. "I have to see to him."

"And I need to leave." He hurried out of the house without saying anything else.

"Fine. That's fine," she muttered as she strode to Jamie's room, a million emotions churning inside her head.

Anger. Desire. Sorrow. Loss. And a sense of discovery with Seth.

Jamie stopped crying when she entered his room and her turmoil subsided. "Hey, baby."

As she lifted him out of his crib he gurgled happily.

She took him to the rocker and cradled him as she nursed him.

He was two months old, she realized as she stroked his soft cheek. Even in the midst of one thing after another for so long, here was her peace.

Holding Jamie.

Albeit her feelings for Seth weren't peaceful. He made her feel happy, secure, confused, guilty.

Maybe he was right. Maybe she needed to deal with her guilt.

She loved Jay. Some part of her always would.

As she rocked their son, she struggled to picture the life she thought they'd have.

She wiped her eyes, just then realizing she was crying. Jamie fussed as she brushed away her tears, and put him to her other breast.

She tried to stop crying, but couldn't.

Somehow she had to let go of the might-have-beens. She had to let go of the future she'd thought they'd have—a future filled with milestones, like their wedding and Jamie's birth, as well as ordinary, everyday days.

She let those images roll through her imagination. One last goodbye to a future that might have been. A future that ended when Jay had died.

Now, she was left to start a new life, to build a new future. And she knew where she had to start. Still, she waffled, knowing what she should do, but not wanting to. And in the midst of that waffling she felt a new surge of annoyance directed at Seth. He was right, and she wasn't happy he was right.

In the end, she called the Martins the next morning and asked if she could stop in. She held her breath as she waited for the answer, hoping that Mrs. Martin had plans that would give her a reprieve, but she wasn't that lucky.

An hour later, she was with them. It was still bitterly cold, so Jamie was in his thick snowsuit and hat, and she'd put a blanket over him. She was thinking that she'd managed to juggle the baby and the diaper bag like an old pro when Mrs. Martin welcomed them into her home.

"Laura, come in. Is that my grandson buried there?" she teased.

"Would you like to unwrap him while I take my things off?"

"I will never turn down an opportunity to hold my grandson." She took the baby and began peeling off the covers and then the snowsuit.

"Hey, Jamie," Mrs. Martin crooned. Her joy was present in her smile, in her every gesture.

Laura felt tears well in her eyes.

Mrs. Martin looked up. "Laura, honey? Is something wrong?"

"No. Not really."

Mrs. Martin carried Jamie and hustled Laura into the living room.

Laura studied all of Jay's pictures. Jay at three months, his high school graduation, and at his swearing in ceremony at City Hall. She lingered at the baby picture. "Jamie looks like Jay."

"He does. I was going to ask if you'd mind my having his picture taken at three months, too. I'd like to keep up the tradition."

"That would be nice." There was a picture of her on the wall, too. Mr. Martin had taken it the day they announced their engagement. She was laughing as she flashed her ring finger in front of the camera.

They'd kept her picture up.

She'd been here with Jamie several times, but she'd never noticed that. There was also a picture of her holding Jamie, and one of the Martins holding him, as well.

"Laura, honey, tell me."

She turned to the woman holding Jamie. Her concern was evident.

"I asked my minister yesterday about Jamie's baptism. We'll do it next month on St. Patrick's Day."

Mrs. Martin smiled. "Jay's favorite holiday of the year. Do you remember the year he dyed his hair green?"

Laura nodded. "His buddy said it would wash right out. But not so much."

"His hair had a green cast to it for weeks." She paused and said, "I can remember that now and laugh. That's a big step."

It was. "I've been writing down stories about Jay for Jamie. Remembering those good times is easier for me, too."

"I have Jay's baptismal gown, if you'd like that for Jamie."

"That would be wonderful. I started to think about that, about things like godparents, and who I wanted to be there for Jamie, I realized I needed to name guardians for him. Mrs. Martin, I can't think of any better guardians for my son if something happened to me than you and Mr. Martin, if you're willing."

"Laura, I'm sure nothing's going to happen—"

Laura cut her off. "No, you're not sure. No one's sure. We didn't think Jay would..." She stopped.

"Die." Mrs. Martin snuggled the baby closer. "You can say it. *I* can say it now. I know that at the time, I went a little crazy and I'm so sorry."

"Mrs. Martin, I understand that better now. Not that I didn't feel the pain when he was sick, I did. I loved him. Jay was my everything."

"About the hospital, Laura. Now that you have Jamie, maybe you understand now. I don't know that you loved Jay any more than we did, but I know in my heart you didn't love him any less."

"Mrs. Martin, I came to apologize to you. I—"

Jay's mother held up a hand. "You have nothing to apologize for, Laura. You loved my son and made him happy, and you've given me a beautiful grandson. But I need to apologize. I understand the decision you wanted me to make in the hospital. I let you down, I'm sorry for that. I'm sorry for the words I said in the midst of my pain. Things I never meant."

Laura didn't know what to say. Her anger was gone and she wasn't sure what to put in its place.

"I like to think that Jay knew I could never make the decision to turn off the ventilator and that's why he left, despite my attempts to keep him," Mrs. Martin said softly. "It was always the same, I was forever wanting to hold on to him a little longer than I should have. That was the thing about my son—he was always willing to help those he loved do what was best, even when they fought against it."

"Mrs. Martin, I don't know what I'd do if it was Jamie. It was a horrible decision to have to make and you did the best you could. I understand that now. Then, I was so angry. Angry at Jay for leaving me. Angry that our plans for our life would never come to fruition. Angry I was left to raise our son alone. Angry Jay would never hold his baby..." She couldn't go on. She burst into tears. "I think I needed that anger to sustain me through the pregnancy and the birth. I couldn't be mad at Jay, so that left you. You and Mr. Martin."

Mrs. Martin was crying as hard as Laura was. "Laura, no matter what I've said, you are my daughter because I've loved you since Jay brought you into our lives. We'd like to be your family, if you'll have us."

Laura was crying so hard that she couldn't answer. She simply hugged Mrs. Martin, sandwiching Jamie between them. Both women sobbed and held each other for a very long time. And when Laura found her voice again, she whispered the words she'd planned on saying after her wedding, "Thank you...Mom."

Which led to renewed tears. This time they weren't tears of grief or regret. They were the tears of joy. Of family finding family.

She thought of the Kellers and realized this was a Homecoming, too.

A while later, after they'd both composed themselves, Mrs. Martin spoke. "Laura, I know our relationship is different than it was. I know we're going to have to find our footing. And I don't want to risk that by speaking out of turn."

"I think we both have reached a place where we can say what needs to be said."

"Then please take this in the spirit in which it is meant," Mrs. Martin said. "It's about Seth."

"He's a friend, ma'am." Laura knew the words were a lie even as she said them.

She thought about what he'd said so matter-of-factly at her house. He loved her. She couldn't say the same to him then, or even think about doing so now.

As if she'd read her thoughts, Mrs. Martin said, "Oh, there's more than that between you, even if neither of you have admitted it."

"I—"

"I'm not asking, Laura. But I wanted to say that if there is more or if it becomes more, if you and Seth find there are feelings between you, it won't hurt us. It won't make us think any less of your love for Jay."

"I loved Jay with my whole heart. I don't know if I can love Seth the way he deserves, Mrs. Martin."

"Mom. Remember."

"Mom." The word felt foreign, but sweet. She'd been without a mother since she was nine and hadn't understood how much she'd wanted Mrs. Martin to fill that void. "I know Seth means a lot to me. He's become my best friend. But I don't know if I love him...at least not like that." Again she thought about him saying he loved her without needing or expecting her to say it back.

"Or maybe you don't know you love him *yet.* Love doesn't come at convenient times. It happens when it happens. We simply wanted you to know that if you do love Seth, or when you're ready to acknowledge it, we'll be all right with it. And I think if my son could pick a man to raise his son, he'd choose a man like Seth Keller."

"Mom."

They both burst into tears again. "Women are a mystery to me," Mr. Martin said from the doorway. "But I hope these are happy tears."

Laura got up from the couch, hurried to the doorway and threw her arms around Jay's father. "Do you mind if I call you Dad now?"

He hugged her back fiercely. "I'd be honored, Laura."

Laura had a headache from all the crying, but her heart felt lighter, so she didn't mind. They planned the baptism, and had to get a new box of tissues.

"I asked Seth to be the godfather."

Both Martins nodded, but Mrs. Martin gave her a see-I-was-right look.

It was close to seven when Laura bundled up Jamie again. Mr. Martin insisted on going out and starting up her car. That left her and Jay's mother alone in the hall.

Mrs. Martin said, "My son gave me so many happy memories, and he gave me you. You can't shake us, Laura."

"I wouldn't want to...Mom."

As she stood at the window and watched Mr. Martin brushing the snow from the car's windshield, she knew she wasn't alone.

She had Jamie and the Martins. She had friends. She had students. Then there was JT. And finally there was Seth.

She didn't lump him in with friends. He was more than that.

The question was, how much more?

CHAPTER THIRTEEN

LOVE.

The word kept coming into Laura's mind the next day. She couldn't shake it. She wanted to talk to Seth—with her best friend—but couldn't. Not yet. She knew she had one more thing to do.

She considered going alone, but in the end, she dressed Jamie and loaded him into the car seat.

They drove west on Twenty-Sixth Street. She went past the funeral home, her favorite restaurants, the park, even the church where Jamie would be baptized.

She drove to Laurel Hill Cemetery on the west side of town. Jay's parents had a plot next to his grandparents', and that's where they'd buried him. Laura hadn't visited the grave since the day of Jay's funeral. Seeing his name on the headstone had seemed too daunting.

But today, she needed to see it.

She remembered being here for the internment. Walking up the slight hill, across the pristine green lawn and canopied by branches of leaves. Now, the ground was covered by a foot of snow, and the trees' branches were barren.

She made her way up the hill, careful of her footing as she held the baby. There was Jay's grandparents' headstone. Alexander Martin and Louisa Bently Martin. Next to it was a smaller headstone that read, *Jameson "Jay" Alexander Martin, Jr.*

Beloved son, husband and father.

Husband.

They'd never officially married, but his parents had acknowledged what she'd known in her heart—if love and commitment meant anything, Jay had been her husband.

She'd loved him.

"I don't believe you're here, but I do believe you can hear me, Jay. I wanted—no needed—to say goodbye. I needed you to know I loved you and that I'll tell our son about you. He will know that even though you never met him, you loved him. I'll look after your parents, too, Jay. You left me a family. Thank you for that. I needed to come here and say goodbye."

She reached in her pocket and took out a small piece of beach glass. Jay had found it on their first date when they'd gone to the peninsula to watch the sunset.

It felt right to leave some tangible sign of her visit, and of her farewell.

She brushed off the headstone with her gloved hand and set the glass token there.

"Goodbye, Jay."

LAURA WENT RIGHT BACK HOME and put Jamie down for his nap. JT arrived after school, and they worked on her homework together at the kitchen counter, just like always. It was the same things she'd done for so many days, but today, everything felt different.

"Ms. Watson?" JT asked.

"Sorry. I was woolgathering."

"Huh?" JT asked.

"Zoning?" Laura tried.

JT laughed. "You do work at growing my vocabulary."

"That's nicer than saying I'm so old I speak an entirely different form of English."

"Well..." JT grinned.

"Okay, I'm back, so let's get to work."

"Actually, I have something to show you, if I can use your laptop."

Curious, Laura got the laptop and booted it up, then slid it toward JT.

JT tapped at the keyboard and slid it back to Laura, who immediately recognized the school's homepage and more specifically, the grading feature. Teachers were urged to enter students' grades within a week of a test or graded homework assignment. The idea was that keeping up on grades allowed the students and faculty to more readily step in if action was needed.

She looked at JT's current grades.

"They're all strong C's, except for math and art class, which are both B's."

"Math's a high B," Laura corrected.

"Yeah. There's a big test in humanities, and I've been studying. I thought we could concentrate on that, and if I can do well on it, I might be able to get that to a B, too."

"JT, this is amazing." Laura looked at the girl. JT still had numerous piercings, and her hair was still super short, but beneath all that was a girl with newfound confidence. "You've worked so hard, and it shows."

JT smiled. "Is the lieutenant coming today? I wanna show him, too."

"I'm not sure—"

"Oh." JT's face fell.

"Let me text him and see." Laura texted, *JT really wants to show you something, if you can stop by.*

Be there soon, was his almost immediate reply.

"He's coming."

Meanwhile, they reviewed JT's humanities work. JT read the chapter out loud, and Laura noticed how much easier she found it. She did struggle a bit, but not as much as she had in the fall. Soon, she'd be cruising.

Laura liked to think her art classes gave her students the foundation for expressing themselves. Reading was akin to that.

She and JT made flashcards for the upcoming test. Picking out important facts in the chapter, they then ran through them once.

"I missed less than half without really studying."

"So, just imagine what you'll be able to do if you study?"

"Thanks, Ms. Watson. I know I have a lot of work left, but for the first time ever, I feel like I can do it. I feel like I'm not stupid anymore."

"JT, you never were. With all your moving around when you were little, it's like...it's like someone gave you a canvas, but no paint. You didn't have all the tools you needed. Now you do."

"Well, not quite. I think maybe I have some of the paint, but I want the rest and I'll still need some brushes."

It was anything but the best analogy on either of their parts, but they both laughed.

Seth came into the room, dressed in his uniform, a small bag in his hand. "Sorry. I knocked, but no one answered so I let myself in. I knew you were expecting me. I had court this afternoon. I'm heading home to catch a nap before third shift."

"No problem, Seth. We're just happy to see you. JT has something to show you."

He glanced at the flashcards and JT followed his line of sight. "Not those. This."

She toggled the laptop's mouse and the grades popped back on to the screen. "Look."

Seth leaned in between them.

Laura was overwhelmed by his scent. It was spicy and warm. She wasn't sure what the name of his cologne was, or if it was simply his soap...or if it was just him. But she missed it. She missed so much about him.

She missed their talks.

She missed sharing her day with him, and missed him sharing his with her.

She missed the feel of him.

She missed seeing him hold Jamie.

She simply missed Seth Keller.

It had only been a few days of him playing the hero and staying away for her sake, but...

"JT, this is terrific," Seth said encouragingly.

How could she not miss someone who reveled in the success of a girl he'd taken under his wing? A man who stayed with a woman giving birth, even though it must have reminded him of what he lost? A man who set up Skype accounts for star-crossed young lovers?

How could she not love him?

"Yeah, it is terrific." JT glowed. "The flashcards are for my humanities test. If I do well on it, that C+ could be a B–. I know they're not Ivy League grades, but—"

"Don't. Don't you belittle what you've accomplished. You've come so far since I met you. You've done so much. You can do anything. Absolutely anything, JT."

"Sometimes, I believe that."

"Anytime you forget, you let me know and I'll remind you. But looking at those grades, you're starting to believe in yourself, too. Soon you won't need us." He glanced at his watch. "I said I'd come in early tonight, so I've got to run or I'll be late." He started toward the door.

"Be right back, JT," Laura said as she rushed after him. "Seth."

He stopped and turned around.

Now that she had his attention, she didn't know what to say. "Could we get together when you have a day off, or in the morning after your shift?"

He glanced at his watch again. "I'm heading home to get some shuteye before I have to go back in to work. I'll call you tomorrow morning." He started to leave, but Laura didn't want him to. She gripped his arm and stood on tiptoe to kiss him. It wasn't nearly as hot as some of the kisses they'd shared. Rather, it was a simple reminder that he mattered to her.

He turned back to the door. "Tomorrow. I'll call you tomorrow."

Laura watched Seth through the window. He got in his truck and sat there, staring at the house.

She wondered what he was thinking.

Hell, she wondered what she was thinking.

She'd said goodbye to Jay and made amends with the Martins. All that was left was admitting what she wanted. She didn't need to figure it out, because she knew. What she wanted had just walked out the door.

JT came into the foyer. "Ms. Watson, Jamie's gurgling on the baby monitor. Can I go get him?"

"Sure. Thanks, JT."

Soon, JT was with the laughing baby. "He really likes me."

"Of course he does."

"Do you think, sometime, if you need someone to watch him, I could? I'll be fifteen in a few months, and I—"

"JT, you don't have to sell me on the idea. There are only a handful of people I could leave Jamie with comfortably, and you are one of them."

"Thanks, Ms. Watson. I mean it. Can I show you something else?"

"Anything, JT."

They went back into the kitchen and JT reached, one-handed, into her bag and thrust a piece of paper at Laura. "I wrote this on the computer, like you said, and the spell-check helped, like you said it would. Of course, there were a few times even it couldn't figure out what word I was trying for."

"It will get easier." Laura unfolded the piece of paper and remembered that night at the police station when JT had handed her the drawing for Jamie's mural.

She didn't know it at the time, but that night was the start of all this. Of the new life she was building for herself. A new life that included Seth Keller.

She read the words on the paper.

Belief
By JT Thomas

I always thought I was stupid. The other kids got what the teachers said, but me, I didn't. They could copy their homework from the blackboard, but I couldn't because I didn't know how to read the words. I could read some. I knew the girl's bathroom from the boy's. I could read small words. But I couldn't read a book, or even my homework. And every year, I felt dumber and the teachers thought I was dumber, too. Then I had a teacher who figured out I couldn't read well. Her and this cop. I told them to leave me alone, but they wouldn't. They kept bugging me and saying I wasn't stupid and they believed in me. And I started to believe in me, too. Sometimes when it's too hard to believe in yourself, it's good to have someone else believe for you.

"JT, that's wonderful."

"Will you check it and give it back to me so I can fix it? I had to do an essay for Mrs. Lutz on myself and I want to make sure it's right before she gets it."

"Sure."

"Thanks, Ms. Watson."

"That's my job, JT." Laura read the essay again, marking it as she went along.

"Glad it's someone's. My mom never cared."

"I'm sure—"

"You've met my mom. She cares about herself more than she'll ever care about me. I wish it was different, but I've decided that's her problem, not mine. Same with Mrs. Lutz. I can't change anyone, but me. You showed me that."

"JT—"

"I went and talked to my guidance counselor. If I work hard and my reading gets better, I'll be able to pass this year, even with the bad first term. But I want more than passing. I want to get my GPA up enough to get into college. Something I never thought I'd do. I figured once I was done with high school, that would be it. But he's looking for programs for me, things I can take over the summer. He said he liked my initiative."

"I do, too."

"Well, I wanted to say thank you for believing in me. You and the lieutenant, you make a good team." JT smiled and added, "You're both big nags."

"Hmm."

There was the sound of a horn in the driveway.

"That's my mom. Gotta run. I got tons of homework to do tonight, and when I'm done, I have this new idea for a mixed-medium collage I want to do."

Laura handed her the corrected essay. "Call if you run into any snags."

"I will."

JT ran to the door and called out, "Hey, Ms. Watson, you got company."

What on earth? Her house had become Grand Central Station.

Eli's friend Tucker was here. Despite the snow, she was still only wearing a hooded sweatshirt. This one proclaimed, *I Deal With Dipsticks For a Living...And I Work With Them, Too.*

Laura laughed. "Great sweatshirt."

Tucker looked down and laughed. "Yeah, I had it made for Christmas. Then I had sweatshirts that simply said, *Dipstick*, made for all the guys in the shop."

"I'm sure they appreciated that." She motioned Tucker to the living room. "Come on in."

"When you're the only woman in a shop full of men, you have to have a sense of humor. I probably shouldn't have just dropped in, but I was making a part run and had this—" she thrust a bag out "—for Jamie. It has nontoxic paint, so even if he gnaws on it, it's okay. Bart had a ton, and loved them."

Laura looked in the paper bag and found a wooden car painted with an intricate design. *Jammin' Jamie*, it read.

Laura sniffed, fighting back tears.

"Laura, is anything wrong?"

"Wrong? What could be wrong? One year ago, I had my whole life planned. And then everything went nuts. I found out I was pregnant. We moved up the wedding. Jay died. I lost his parents. And then there's Seth. Seth who was as lost without Allie as I was without Jay. He was my friend when I needed a friend—someone who didn't know me and Jay together. Someone who didn't give me those pitying looks. Seth understood what I was going through. And then he turns everything around on me."

"What did he do?" Tucker asked, looking as if things might go badly for Seth if she didn't like the answer.

"He said he loved me. That he knew I was still mourning and he'd wait until I was ready."

"Seth's right."

"What?"

"You need to take your time and mourn Jay, but he wouldn't expect you to be alone."

"How can I love someone else so soon?"

"How can you not? If I know anything about the Keller family it's that they're impossible to resist. They Kellerize you and before you even know what's happening, you find you can't live without them."

"Did you ever have feelings for one of them?"

Tucker cut her off with a bark of laughter. "Oh, no. I mean, I love the Kellers—all the Kellers, but not any of the guys like that. You, on the other hand, have been in love with Seth for a long time. Eli tells me I'm the most obtuse person in the world when it comes to reading people, so if I can see that, how can *you* not?"

"Maybe it's not the seeing it. Maybe it's the admitting it."

"Hey, when I was pregnant, I knew I was pregnant, but I couldn't admit it. I was scared to death. I went to Eli and told her what I thought. Saying the words made a difference—they made it real. Once I'd said, 'I'm pregnant,' I could deal with it. So, Laura, are you in love with Seth?"

Laura didn't say anything for a moment. Then she nodded. "Yes." And with that one word, it was as if everything got clearer. "Yes. I love Seth."

"Nice. But maybe you should tell him, not me?"

She nodded. "You're right."

"Yeah, like I tell the guys at the shop, always being right is a curse, but one I've learned to live with." Tucker shrugged. "Hey, I'll leave and let you decide what to do next."

What to do next? Find Seth and tell him.

Third shift started at ten, so he had hours before he reported back to the station. If she was lucky she could catch him before he went in, because she wasn't sure she could wait until tomorrow to tell him.

Now that she'd said the words out loud, she was impatient to say them again, this time to Seth. She called Mrs. Martin, who came and got Jamie for the evening. She didn't even ask what

Laura had to do. She just patted her hand and said, "Take your time, honey."

"Thanks, Mom," Laura had responded. It came easier this time. Mom. She had a family.

Laura knew that this confession would need something special, and with sudden surety, she knew just what it required. It took an hour and a half of prep time, but as Laura got organized she caught herself singing JoJo's "Coming for You," and when she realized that she was not only singing, but what she was singing, she laughed with the sheer joy of it.

She loved Seth Keller.

And it didn't mean she no longer loved Jay.

She knew that Seth didn't love Allie less.

But love wasn't about mores or lesses—it just was. There was no limit on love, the heart grows exponentially. Laura agreed.

And she needed to get to Seth and explain. She was just pulling on her boots when someone knocked on the door.

Why had her house become the destination of choice in Erie? She didn't want to be rude, but she was going to have to get rid of whoever was here. Her desire to see Seth was increasing by the second.

She opened the door and found Seth standing there. "Seth, I was just getting ready to come to your place." She pointed at her one booted foot, and her other socked one. "I need to talk to you."

"Shh."

"Shh?" she asked.

"Yes, shush, Laura. I want to say something, and I don't want you interrupting." He stepped into the foyer and she shut the door.

"I talked to a friend at work," he began, "Chuck had fallen for a woman who'd been burned by love and kept saying she wasn't ready to get involved. He didn't listen and made a big event out of telling her how he felt. I thought I would wait patiently for you to figure out we're meant to be together, but I was wrong. The last few days I've managed to stay away have been horrible. I need you. And I decided Chuck was right, that I should take a lesson from my teenage self. When you find love, you grab on to it, and don't waste a minute of it. I didn't think you were big on public events, but I wanted you to know how I felt, so I made a list."

"List?" she asked.

He reached into his coat pocket and pulled out a Post-it. "I know it's not Thanksgiving, but I don't think being thankful should fall on only one day of the year."

Laura looked down and read the Post-it. *I'm thankful that not only has life given me a second chance, but so has love.* She met his gaze, ready to tell him the words she'd been so afraid to say. She wanted to shout them to Seth—to the world.

"Laura, let me finish. I know it's too soon for you. That getting over losing someone takes time. So I want you to know that I'm here. For as long as it takes. I love you. You are my list. You,

Jamie and my family. I'm holding on and not letting go. Ever."

"Am I unshushed now?"

Seth's nervousness was clear. "Yes."

"Remember the day Eli and Zac brought Ebony home?"

"Sure."

"Homecoming. Of all the reasons you Kellers have to gather, those are the most significant, right?" He nodded.

She took his hand, which felt so right in hers, and led him into the kitchen. "This isn't quite as elegant as a Keller Homecoming speech, but it's just as heartfelt. The Martins, they're my family, not simply Jamie's grandparents. That realization was a Homecoming of sorts. I am not alone."

On the counter was a covered dish. Laura removed the foil wrapping to unveil a homemade cake.

Welcome Home, Seth, it read in icing. "I'm not talking about a place, but about a feeling. We both loved people before. Really loved them. That doesn't mean we can't love someone else. I had parents I adored, but they're gone. Now I have Jay's parents. And I have you. I love you, Seth. You are my home. Mine and Jamie's."

She didn't wait for Seth's response, but threw herself into his embrace and kissed him. She tried to put everything she hadn't said with the elegance that a Keller might have into that kiss. She loved him. She needed him. She wanted him.

Seth released her and smiled. "I love you, too."

With that said, they sat at the kitchen table and decided to take it one day at a time. They wouldn't rush marriage, but they were committed. It wasn't the life that either of them expected, but it would be a good one. Filled with family, friends and most importantly, love.

"Welcome home, Laura," Seth said, his arms open wide.

EPILOGUE

DEAR JAMIE,
Today was St. Patrick's Day. Your father, Jay, loved this day. He was Irish, but even if he wasn't, he'd have claimed he was on March 17 each year. I started a memory box for you, and one of the things in it is a well-worn St. Patrick's Day T-shirt—it was his favorite.

Today was also your Baptism. You didn't cry once. I was so proud as Seth and JT promised to serve as your godparents.

After your father died, I was worried about being alone. But as I looked out at the pews, they were filled with people. Your grandparents, the police officers who worked with your father, the entire Keller family. There are a lot of them.

But that's probably a good thing, since Seth asked me to marry him and I said yes.

We've decided on a long engagement. But I have no doubts. Neither does he.

I loved your father with all my heart and was afraid I'd never love anyone that way again. And I won't—not the same way. I love Seth in an entirely different, but equally special way. He's a part of myself that I never knew I was missing.

Jamie, you are surrounded by love. You may only know your father through these journals, and through the stories we'll tell you, but never doubt he loved you. And I like to think he had a hand in helping us both find Seth.

When Seth came to the house with that "list" I realized that life gives second chances…but now I know that sometimes, so does love.
Love,
Mom

~~~~

Dear Reader,

If you're a regular reader of my books, did you catch the small shout-out to Chuck from *Once Upon a Valentine's*? I so enjoyed writing my PTA Mom trilogy. I've lived a PTA Mom life! And I love sneaking old characters into new books! Speaking about new books, thank you for picking up *Homecoming*, the third book in my *Hometown Hearts* series. I hope you enjoyed the story. If you did, *please* leave a review at your favorite online store. It's the best way to help new readers discover my books. And I hope you'll watch for the fourth story in my *Hometown Hearts* series, *Suddenly a Father*. In a small town like Whedon, you're bound to run into someone you know!

Holly

Hometown Hearts
1. Crib Notes
2. A Special Kind of Different
3. Homecoming
4. Suddenly a Father
A Hometown Hearts Wedding
5. Something Borrowed
6. Something Blue
7. Something Perfect

ABOUT THE AUTHOR

Award-winning author Holly Jacobs has over three million books in print worldwide. The first novel in her Everything But... series, *Everything But a Groom*, was named one of 2008's Best Romances by Booklist, and her books have been honored with many other accolades. She lives in Erie, Pennsylvania, with her husband and four children. You can visit her at *www.HollyJacobs.com*

www.ingramcontent.com/pod-product-compliance
Lightning Source LLC
Chambersburg PA
CBHW020047180626
46812CB00006B/2225